M000012976

ADVANCE PRAISE FOR
THE WEIGHT OF ASHES

"*The Weight of Ashes* is such a wild ride! When it finally takes a break from all that page-turning action, it's to remind us of the inevitability of that moment of shared experience – the feeling we haven't grown up quite yet, but we're not kids anymore, either. It's a visceral, pulse-pounding look at our desperation to keep things the same even as real life is letting us know that's impossible. You won't be able to avoid being dragged back to your childhood in the best way possible."
– Chris Negron, author of *Dan, Unmasked* and *The Last Super Chef*

"A boy does not accept the death of his beloved older brother. To him, love is every bit as strong as death. The adventure in *The Weight of Ashes* is a rollercoaster, a descent into a child's almost mad heart even as the novel climbs on wheels of insight and loving prose. It's an unlikely, yet all so human, journey between grief and faith."
– David L. Robbins, *New York Times* bestselling author of *Isaac's Beacon* and *War of the Rats*

"Filtered through a phantasmal lens of lost innocence, Zachary Steele roots his stunning novel in a childhood mythology of grief and healing akin to Stephen King's haunting novella, *The Body*."
– Clay McLeod Chapman, author of *The Remaking* and *Whisper Down the Lane*

"With a pinch of *Stand by Me* and dash of delicious nostalgia for childhood before smartphones, *The Weight of Ashes* is a page-turning coming-of-age story about one boy's quest to end his grief after the death of his brother. Steele immerses you in dense settings as he takes you on Mark's journey through the woods to find the witch who can bring Mitch back. With a compelling cast of characters painted across a canvas that blends urban legend and reality, it's a gripping story from beginning to end."
– Ricki Cardenas, author of *Switch & Bait*

THE WEIGHT OF ASHES

ZACHARY STEELE

This is a work of fiction. Names, characters, places, and incidents either are the product of the author's imagination or are used fictitiously. Any resemblance to actual events, locales, organizations, or persons living or dead, is entirely coincidental and beyond the intent of either the author or the publisher.

The Story Plant
Studio Digital CT, LLC
P.O. Box 4331
Stamford, CT 06907

Copyright © 2021 by Zachary Steele

Story Plant paperback ISBN-13: 978-1-61188-302-2
Fiction Studio Books E-book ISBN: 978-1-945839-51-1

Visit our website at www.TheStoryPlant.com

All rights reserved, which includes the right to reproduce this book or portions thereof in any form whatsoever except as provided by U.S. Copyright Law. For information, address The Story Plant.

First Story Plant Printing: July 2021

Printed in Canada
0 9 8 7 6 5 4 3 2 1

To Benji

For your friendship, dedication, passion, and for talking me down from the ledge far too many times to count.

1

My cousin Gordon drove through the stop sign at sixty miles an hour. His 280z must have looked like a shiny silver bullet chasing its headlights. Mama said the other car was a '66 Buick, built like a tank. I tried hard not to think about what my brother Mitch did in those last few seconds. But it happened anyway.

Probably he didn't scream. Mitch didn't scare easy.

The Buick hit the passenger side so hard it flipped the 280z into a roll off Georgia Highway 9. Gordon was thrown free after his door broke off; he wound up in the grass beside the road with a cracked shoulder blade and only cuts and bruises otherwise. He wasn't wearing a seat belt. I guess that saved his life. Mitch always fastened his belt, always followed the rules. He got on me when I didn't.

Older brothers are supposed to do that.

Mitch died in the wreck, on a Tuesday.

Mama didn't tell me about it until Wednesday. She held me out of school. It was the last week before summer break, so I kinda welcomed it. She took me to the ole rickety church she pretends we go to regularly so she could tell me in front of Reverend Mills, a stranger. I didn't know what she wanted me to say, but I told her and the reverend they were wrong. Mitch wasn't gone. Not for good, anyway.

It started raining that morning, while we were leaving the church. Thunder shook the ground. Mama said the angels were weeping. She stood by the car with her arms wide until she was wet to the bone. Said she wanted to be cleansed by their tears. Then she got in, strapped the seat belt on, and cried while I stared out my window.

There wasn't a viewing. Mama said there wasn't a need for anyone to see Mitch that way. She had him cremated. Reverend Mills encouraged Mama to hold a memorial at the church after the service on Friday. I didn't want to go, but I could hear Mitch telling me to do as she asked. My friends came to support me. I hadn't seen them since the accident. That was when I asked for their help.

I don't know if they believed me then. I didn't need them to, I guess. I just needed them there. I couldn't make the plan work without them. Couldn't do it alone.

Mama kept saying I needed to accept that Mitch was with Jesus. That he was gone. I needed to move on.

I didn't want to.

I wanted my brother back.

2

When I shifted, the pew creaked. Reminded me of a door opening in a haunted house, slow and eerie. Still, it was more comforting than their silence. More comforting than the bleak organ music that filled the sanctuary. Any bit of sound otherwise was crying, most of which came from Traci Stevens. Mascara streaked her face in shades of blue and black. Her cheeks were puffy, blonde hair blasted with hair spray and unlikely to ever move again. I don't know if Traci was ever Mitch's girlfriend, but they were close. Had been for years. A few of her friends formed a tight group around her, while bawling away as if tears were breath. Maybe they knew Mitch. Maybe Traci's sobs got to them. But the commotion certainly made the other kids in the church stare forward as if there was nothing else to look at, blank as could be. Like they were hit by a shoe and weren't sure how to react.

From my pew a few rows from the back, it all looked like a show.

Mama stood near the pulpit, unbalanced and fighting it, decorative white wooden box on a tall oak stand at her side. Mitch's ashes were in there, in a sealed bag. I hadn't looked at them. Didn't need to. From the time she'd picked them up, Mama had kept the box close by, barely letting it down. Even at sleep, she'd set it centered on the dresser at the foot of her bed, where she could see it. Wet trails streaked her cheeks, balled hands tight around a wad of used tissues, shaking slightly; but she looked pretty. It had been a long while since I'd seen her in a dress. This one was black and almost to the floor. I think it was new. I couldn't remember seeing it before.

To her side Reverend Mills loomed, long face working that practiced somber grin he probably learned in Reverend School. People usually bought into it. Somehow felt better no matter what was ailing them. I just wanted him to go away. He'd been trying to talk to me about Mitch every time I was within earshot. Kept feeding Mama lines about Heaven and Mitch being home with Jesus. Buried in his ways, he couldn't possibly understand. He didn't know what I knew.

Mitch always said that was the problem with church folk. They're all just waiting in a line they're not allowed to leave. Just living to die.

He told me to live to live. Stay out of lines. There's more than one road home.

And more than one way to cheat death.

"You're sure about this? I mean, how do you know?"

Reggie was always the first to speak. Not that she talked too much. Just first. Whether you wanted her to or not. I wanted to look at her but couldn't bring myself to. I'd never seen her hair out of pigtails, or not covered by a ball cap. It hung long over her shoulders like black silk, shiny and stark against her pale-blue dress. Her grandma was a full-blooded Cherokee. Reggie got her dark eyes and tanned skin. Despite that, the rosy shade of her cheeks flared like heat, eyes made up. It was stupid, I knew, but it felt like she was in costume. Like she was someone else. She was Regina, a girl I'd never met that made me stupid nervous for some reason. Not the friend I'd had since second grade. The friend I'd spent more alone time with than anyone, no worry over boys and girls and sticky gross feelings that made me sweat. Now my palms were slick no matter how much I rubbed them on the legs of my trousers. So, I just listened and stared at a hymnal tucked in the back of the pew ahead. If I only heard her voice, it was still Reggie.

"Seen it," I said, voice barely above a whisper. "She can do it."

"But how—" Reggie dropped into quiet, fiddled with the fluffy hem of her dress. "Mitch isn't, well, I mean he's not ... How can she even make that happen now?"

Dunk turned a bit her way, his wide frame rocking the entire pew, buttons threatening to pop free of his pinstriped dress shirt. "A phoenix rises from ashes. Why can't Mitch?"

"Yeah, I know, but—" Reggie stopped short again, but she didn't need to finish. I knew what she would have said. She was always good at that kind of thing. Changed direction like a bird in flight. But I knew how she flew. "Spook Hill's a long way. Has to be six miles or so."

"Four. Mitch said it takes about three plus hours by foot, since we have to cut through the woods."

"And if it's still raining?"

"It'll stop." Their stares fell on me heavy. I could only look at Reggie for a flash. Something in the way she looked at me was different. Seemed to probe deeper. Kind of like a look trying to be a hug. It was weird and I didn't like it. Dunk and Mo stayed silent, sitting just past her. Waiting. Smart enough to know she'd talk again before they could anyway. "Saw it on the news."

She didn't let up. She never let up. "Spook Hill's big, Mark. How are we supposed to find her?"

"Map. Mitch drew it. He's good with maps."

For a second, Mo looked ready to say something. His thick lips opened then closed as he pushed his large glasses as high up as they went. The frames were as dark as his skin. Sometimes nearly impossible to see. No words to offer, he pressed his suit, leaned back, and all but vanished behind Dunk. Not a hard thing to do when you're as small as he was. I knew it well. We were both short and scrawny and as easy to miss as a frog with no croaker.

Thunder rattled the stained-glass windows, giving the Kaleidoscope Jesus behind the choir seats a good shake. Traci squealed, then wailed even louder. Another group of people passed through the vestibule and into the sanctuary, on a line down the aisle past us. I steadied my gaze on the cover of the hymnal, unwilling to make eye contact. I didn't want anyone else offering me condolences that weren't necessary.

"I mean, we'll go," said Reggie, giving a good puff of a sigh for effect. "Whatever you need."

Dunk nodded in agreement, round cheeks hot pink and wobbling along. Mo had to lean forward for me to see him doing the same, though with that half smile of his that said he wasn't sold.

Reggie noted Mama with a quick nod. "But she won't be happy with you."

"She'll be happier when I come back with Mitch."

Reggie shifted a touch toward me, our elbows grazing, ready to lower her voice to say something practical I wouldn't want to hear—but a sharp yelp cut her off.

Almost sheltered behind the pulpit, Mama cradled the white box, whispering something to Reverend Mills. Like a soldier on orders, he stepped into the aisle, hand out, palm to the shoulder of a small woman that clearly wanted nothing to do with him. If it had only been her screeching protest, I'd still have known it was Aunt Dawn. Her voice cracked when she screamed—which was often—as if she'd caught a cough that wouldn't quit. Behind her, Gordon backed off, a few easy steps at a time, head on a slow swivel. Gave the impression he was checking to see who was watching. But I knew better. He was looking past everyone. Looking for me. I'd never much cared for the way he stared at me. Especially since the day at the ballfield. Like he was thinking of all the ways he could get back at me for ending his chances at playing professional ball. There, in the commotion of the sanctuary, it gave my heart a skip. Burned me from the inside out. I wanted to hurt him. I wanted Mitch's green Easton bat, so I could finish the job right and crack open Gordon's head.

But I couldn't. He had to be alive or none of it would matter.

Cuts lined Gordon's face and neck, as if he'd gone to war with a feral cat. His left arm was in a sling, same as the one he wore for six weeks after I cracked his shoulder blade in April. He'd only had it free for three weeks. He shouldn't have come. Neither of them should have. *He* was the reason we were there at all.

Aunt Dawn made a wild attempt to force herself around the reverend, who, to his credit, wrapped her up with his long arms and swept her away. "Another time," he said, calm as anything, as if this sort of thing happened all the time. With the exception of Traci and Aunt Dawn, the entire sanctuary had fallen stone silent. But Traci went to bawling louder, as though she'd just heard the news all over again. Like this was about her.

"I need to see her! Let ... me ... go!" Aunt Dawn landed a solid elbow to the reverend's ribs and he buckled, down to a knee, struggling to find a breath as Aunt Dawn bowled him over to get to Mama. "Morgan, please."

Mama turned the white box away in a flash. Climbed the three steps to the stage and backed away, head shaking. "I can't talk to you." Her voice dropped to a whimper, behind a fresh wash of tears. I'd never seen her this way and it drove my temper to boiling hot. "Not right now."

Mitch would have put a stop to it straight off. Would have put himself between Mama and a grizzly. But I didn't move. I just sat there beside my friends, fists clenched, all four of us watching like it was the most intense episode of *The Wonder Years* we'd ever seen.

Aunt Dawn kneeled at the base of the steps, repeated cries of "please" drowned out by sobs. Mama had all but backed into the choir seats. The reverend found his footing, at Aunt Dawn's side at a distance, trying to encourage her away.

Gordon, on the other hand, worked his way up the aisle, away from Aunt Dawn's outburst as if he hardly knew her.

Taking his cue as an opportunity of their own, a few folks rose from the pews and filed out ahead of Gordon. He clipped Mrs. Wilkins' walker and she made a fuss. But her teeth weren't in. Whatever she said was done and over in a hurry. Not that Gordon was listening.

There was a moment when he stopped, hand flipped through his blonde hair, bloodshot blue eyes looking down on me, when I could have sworn he wasn't bothered by any of it. That he could have cared less what happened to Mitch. Could have cared less who it hurt. Maybe I'd known him too long to think otherwise. Mitch always said Gordon carried his heart like it was a grenade.

"Let's talk." His voice was softer than normal, but still sharp and to the point. A quieter version of his mother.

I tried to think of all the things Mitch might say, but in the ruckus I couldn't focus.

"Murph, let's go." He flinched, triggered by another volley of wails from Aunt Dawn. "This place gives me the creeps."

"He doesn't want to talk to you." Dunk stood, filling the aisle, as fast as I'd ever seen him move. His thick arms bowed, fists balled, cheeks red hot. For a thirteen-year-old kid, Dunk was strong. He said it was from working so often at construction with his dad.

"Stuff it, Moresize. Nobody's asking."

"It's Sizemore," shot Reggie, up as well.

The smile on Gordon's face made me sick, as did the way he eyed her.

"Well, well. You *are* a pretty little Indian girl after all, aren't you? If you ever want to be a woman—"

"Go away!" The hymnal flew in a flutter of pages, as much a shock to me as anyone. I didn't even realize I had grabbed it. It collected Gordon's shoulder with a thud. He yelped, nearly drawing his arm free of the sling, only to yell louder as the pain from his shoulder blade kicked in. "This is your fault! And you're going to pay for it!"

Once the worst of the pain subsided, he laughed. A slow and amused chuckle. I wanted to throw up. Did he think it was a joke?

"Pay? What do you think you're going to do, runt nuts?"

Mo moved to block his path but was hardly a match. Gordon shoved him hard to the pew with ease, raised the back of his free hand to strike Dunk clear. That was as far as he got. Aunt Dawn's palm found his cheek with a swipe of her left hand, turned his head in a quick snap. The pop was loud enough to silence the rain. Gordon locked on to me like I was the one who'd hit him.

"In the car. Now." Aunt Dawn's voice emerged all breath, a growl that somehow filled the room. A red welt rose from ear to chin, but Gordon didn't reach for it. He barely reacted at all. Instead he withdrew, backing clear until he dropped from sight.

The fierceness in Aunt Dawn's face faded, skin washed pale, tears streaking rapid. She cast a final look at Mama, then briefly at me like I was supposed to come in for a hug. Then she turned and stormed out. As soon as the door shut behind her, the rain let its breath free and fell heavy once again.

If I wasn't ready before, I was now.

The wrong person was in that oak box.

Mitch deserved better, and I was going to make sure he got it.

"Nine, tomorrow," I said to my friends. "At the Junkyard. We'll head to the Mall from there."

A nod passed from Reggie to Dunk to Mo. Then I worked my way free to tend to Mama.

3

"**M**arkie, baby, get the door."

I wanted to tell her not to call me that anymore, remind her I was a teenager now, but I let it go. Another time. She'd been in her room crying for an hour as it was, and the alcohol had begun to turn her mind. In the days following the accident, it was her daily schedule. Drunk and passed out by ten, asleep until noon. Mama didn't drink much normally. Certainly, never enough to leave her in that state. I didn't like that everything with Mitch had driven her to it, but, in the moment, I hoped for the same. It was the only way I could get to Mitch's ashes.

Family Matters was about to start. It was a re-run, but Urkel reminded me of Mo. Skinny, way smarter than any of us nerds, a bit on the dramatic side—though Mo sang way better and didn't sound like Woody Woodpecker when he laughed. I couldn't watch an episode without smiling about how much Mo rolled his eyes when I made the comparison.

I made my way to the door in a hurry, hoping whoever it was would drop off whatever baked dish they'd brought and go away as fast. The handle jiggled when I turned it, felt like it was going to come loose again, so I slowed enough to make sure it didn't. Mitch wasn't there to fix it. It would have to wait until he was back.

The storm door rattled as the main door opened, scattering moths every which way. Officer John swatted at them, almost knocked his hat free. He was in full uniform. Like always. He said as Sheriff of Boling County he was always on duty. I stared at him through the glass of the storm door a few seconds too long.

"Evening, Mark." The moths were giving him a fit, but he sounded calm about it. "Your mother in?"

He knew she was. The two of them acted like Mitch and I couldn't see what was happening. He was showing up once or more a week months before the accident. Always with some supposed news to pass along to Mama about the church bake sale or talk on Reverend Mills' sermon, or some such baloney. Mama said it was nothing more than a Bible study group. Not that either of them had a Bible out. She'd send us to our room while they talked nonsense a bit. When they thought we'd stopped listening, it got mushy. We didn't try to listen, of course. We'd rather not have heard any of it. But the boombox was the only way we could drown it out, and Mama yelled if we turned it too loud.

Between the double-wide's thin walls and the inch-high gap at the base of our door, we may as well have been in the same room. Mama should have known that much. She was always on to me and Mitch about being quiet at bedtime, and most times we were only whispering.

I put my shoulder into the storm door to pop it free. Officer John tipped his hat and came in. The theme to *Family Matters* had started, but I knew I wasn't going to get to watch it, so I turned the television off as I passed. At Mama's open door, I knocked on the frame before I entered.

The old lamp on Mama's nightstand gave off an orange sort of light through the red shade. Made the dingy walls look like the sky at sunset. The bottle of Jack next to the lamp was nearly half gone. I couldn't remember if there was a new bottle on the stand when we got home, but an empty one rose tall above the rim of her trash. No glass in sight. Curled up on the bed, Mama had wrapped herself in her ratty pink robe, sheets kicked aside, white box snuggled to her chest. If she passed out that way, I'd never pry it free.

I inched closer. Whispered, "It's Officer John."

Mama's face was puffy and red, eyes bloodshot. Even in the muddy light I could tell that much. She didn't move. Just blinked a few times. "I'm in no condition."

Suited me. I would have preferred he left anyway, so I could watch my show. But I eyed that white box and knew it couldn't go down that way.

21

She had to get up. It had to wind up on the dresser. "He's already in the living room."

"You let him in without checking with me first?"

"You told me never to leave him on the porch."

Mama sniffed. Forced a nod into the sheets. "I did. You're right. You're a good boy. You listen so well." When she moved to sit up, I tried to help. But she quickly waved me off and almost tipped over. "I'm a mess. Keep him company. I'll be out in a few. Shut the door on your way."

For a moment I thought she was talking to the box rather than me.

"Want me to put it on the dresser?"

"No, baby. I got it. Go on, now."

Challenging Mama on any occasion was never wise. I knew better than to try it then, no matter how much I wanted to. "Yes, Mama."

Officer John was cozy on the sofa, in the same spot I was sitting in moments before. His gun was holstered, radio microphone clipped to the breast pocket of his gray uniform. This time, he was definitely on duty, which meant he wouldn't stay long. He gave me a wide smile that didn't last. "Mama will be a few minutes," I said as I dropped into the Lay-Z-Boy.

He nodded, patted his knees to some tune in his head, then threw another quick smile my way, upper lip briefly disappearing behind his bushy moustache. A lady's voice blared on the radio, shrill and country, with talk of some suspect they were after around downtown Hogan. He cut the volume low, offered a quick glance as if he was protecting a secret conversation.

When her yammering tale came to a stop, he held for a response, mic gripped tight. A deep drawl barked a quick *nothing yet*, then signed off. "Brice has it," Officer John said, as if I asked.

Things fell silent again. I considered turning the television back on, if only to keep us both from having to speak thoughts neither wanted to, but Mama wouldn't have cared for it. I was supposed to talk to him. The way Mitch did. He could talk to anyone about anything.

"Went to a Braves game with Reggie's family last week." I had no idea what else to say. Mama often said I didn't know there was a world beyond the baseball field. She was right. There wasn't.

"Yeah? Surprised Kenny would spring to take anyone anywhere. Lousy good for—" Officer John caught himself with a smile. Not that it was a secret that Reggie's dad was a bit of an unpleasant type. He barely spoke the whole game, except to hush Reggie when she got to talking too much. "They win?"

I shook my head. "Cubs won, 3-2. Pete Smith pitched all right, I guess, but their guy was better."

"Yeah? Who'd they have?" Officer John sat straight. The smile held this time. I'd never considered he might like baseball. I'd never asked.

"Greg Maddux. Hadn't heard of him, but he was super good. Almost went the whole game. Nobody but Murphy and Thomas got to him."

"Dale Murphy, huh? Your mother said Mitch once convinced you he was your father." Officer John covered his mouth with his hand, said something sharp behind it. He removed his hat and angled my way. "Damn. Sorry, Mark. Didn't mean to bring him up. I'm sorry."

I didn't know what to say, so I shrugged. From Mama's room, the toilet flushed, high-pitched whine fading as it settled. Water splashed in the sink. Hopefully, she wouldn't be much longer.

"It'll be okay, you know."

"I know." And I did. "It'll be fine tomorrow." The words were out before I realized it.

"What?"

"Nothing."

Officer John held a stare on me for longer than I was comfortable. The policeman's stare. Finally, he offered a nod. "It just takes time. Dealing with loss isn't easy, I know. Lost my share of folks over the years. None hit me as hard as losing Boomer, though. My dog when I was a kid. My best friend. Would have given anything to have him back. Almost did. Loss brings on a lot of hurt you can't shake. Maybe never do. But you just have to face it. Learn to accept it. Everything will be fine again. I promise."

I wanted him to drop it, but I could tell he meant well. He was always nice to me and Mitch, good around Mama; and at least she was willing to get out of bed and look presentable for him.

The plan aside, it was good she had someone that got her moving. "Thanks."

After that, the quiet returned. Officer John busied himself looking anywhere but at me, while I bounced my feet on the foot of the closed recliner. I tried to think what Mitch would say but couldn't get much past baseball. I knew some about movies, and television, and music. But Mitch knew about a lot more.

Fortunately, Mama saved me the worry. Her door popped open and she came out in jeans and a pretty white blouse. Somehow, in just a few minutes, she'd cleaned up nice. Hair pulled back in a tight ponytail, her face less puffy, colored and made up. It was hard to even tell she'd been crying. I don't know how she did it. Took me half an hour to get ready for school, and all I had to do was brush my teeth and hair and throw on some clothes.

"Evening, John." Mama leaned into the door frame, head rested against the chipped wood.

Officer John jumped to his feet like something bit him, large round hat off and all but pressed into his chest. "Evening, Morgan. Heard about the service. Wanted to stop by and make sure you're all right."

Mama offered him a smile, but I could tell the tears were building just thinking about it. Aunt Dawn had called three times after we got home. Mama wouldn't answer. She finally told me to unplug the phone. When she turned her attention my way, it was like watching the clock tick down to the last bell at school. I was already set to go.

"Markie, baby, go to your room. I need a moment with John."

Most times I'd fuss over it. Only television was in the living room. There wasn't much more than toys and games to keep me busy in the bedroom. Especially without Mitch there. I could think of a thousand places I'd have rather been than that empty room. But there were things I needed to do to get ready for the journey in the morning, so I was glad to be free of whatever brought Officer John by. I all but leaped out of the chair.

"Good seeing you, Mark," said Officer John. "Enjoyed the talk."

It brought me to a stop. Officer John was nice, and I was glad he could be there for Mama. When she noticed me looking back, she broke her stare on him. Her smile faded, and she flinched as if I caught her doing wrong. Mitch wouldn't have let her feel so uncomfortable about things. I didn't want her to either. "We're okay with it. The two of you. So you know." Before they could respond, I hurried into the room and closed the door.

Mitch's bed was made, the narrow twin mattress covered snug and tight, ball glove in the center, ball in the webbing. I'd never been as good at keeping my bed neat. Mitch kept showing me how to do it proper, but I couldn't get the corners right. For a few seconds, I forgot what had happened and expected he'd come in soon to give me grief about it. Then it hit me that he wouldn't be home, same as he hadn't been the past three nights, and I choked up. My breath shortened.

"He'll be home tomorrow," I reminded my-self, opening and closing a few dresser drawers, though I wasn't looking for anything. "Everything will be normal again tomorrow."

My breath slowed.

"Just like it was before."

4

The ball nearly touched the ceiling, an inch or two from raining plaster down on Mitch as he lay on his bed. But he never hit it. He knew distance like a dog sensed a storm. I swear he had a radar in his brain. As if ordered to obey, the ball stopped short, hovered a split second, red-stitched seams spinning a turn, then dropped into his waiting glove.

It landed with a soft tap in the worn leather. Despite the crumpled look of it, the way it flopped about as if barely held together, Mitch could snap that glove to attention with the slightest twitch of his fingers. In a flash, he had the ball again, palmed tight as he craned his arm beside his head. Then he let it go with the flick of a wrist, fingers pointing to the spot he wanted it to go. The spot it always went.

It was mesmerizing.

I'd tried it once when Mitch wasn't home. About put a hole in the ceiling and spent the next three days finding bits of ceiling debris in my sheets.

"Crazy Train" kicked in, and somehow Mitch managed to dial the boombox up a notch without losing any rhythm to his ball toss. His eyes shifted to the door—he still caught the ball of course—waiting, listening, head nodding to the beat of the guitar. When Mama's voice didn't come, he gave me a wink and went back to watching the ball.

It wasn't yet March, so baseball season was still a month away, but I sat on the edge of my bed, oiling my glove all the same. Sometimes it seemed that first practice, the first step on the field, would never get there. When it was properly oiled, I put a ball in the pocket and wrapped a belt tight around the glove.

"Gonna be another train wreck of a season," Mitch said, popping the ball once in the mitt before tossing it again. "Can't see anyone other than your daddy doing much good for the Braves this year."

I crossed my arms and tried to give him that look Mama gave us that said, "Don't test me," but I couldn't hold back a smile.

"Still can't believe you fell for that," he said, then laughed.

"I was five. Would have believe anything you told me."

"You still do."

"No, I don't," I shot back, even though I knew different. Of course I did. I'd have believed him if he told me we really lived on Mars.

Ozzy Osborne's strange singing voice cut through Mitch's laugh. I gave my words some thought before speaking. I'd never asked before and I wasn't sure what Mitch would say. "You ever miss him?"

"Dale Murphy?" Mitch's face scrunched up, head rolled my way.

This time I didn't have to try to make the look. It made itself. "You know who I mean."

Mitch rolled back, ball drawn from the glove and tossed as quick. "Yeah, I know. Didn't know him all that well, though. I mean, I was three when you were born, right? What did I know about anything? But he's the one who ran off and left Mama and us. Can't give him too much care for that. Sometimes I still miss him. Probably always will. Just the way it is."

I lay on my side, legs tucked up until I could wrap my arms around them at the knees. "I wonder what it'd be like to have a father."

The ball dropped into his glove. Mitch held a second or two, then took the mitt off and set it on the floor. He sat up and leaned forward, eyes heavy on me. Connected to me. "You don't need a father, bro. You got me."

When he smiled, I smiled with him.

Then he stood, made like he was stretching, but I knew what was coming. Knew there wasn't anything I could do to stop it. Knew I really didn't want to stop it.

In a leap, he was on me, bed groaning a protest, his fingers working like mad against my ribs. Got me laughing so hard I thought I'd pee myself. But he knew how far to take it. When to stop.

Maybe cause he'd gone too far once years before and I'd soaked the mattress. Mama had reamed him out good for that.

He was back on his feet before I knew it, the tickle lingering even without his touch. He clapped his hands and rubbed them together, greedy as Snidely Whiplash plotting an attack.

"We've gotta figure out our movie schedule. *Major League* and that *Field of Dreams* flick are both coming out next month. Can you imagine? Two baseball movies in the same month? We have to see 'em both. You and me, right?"

For so many reasons I couldn't count, a smile stretched the length of my face until I thought that was all I could possibly be.

"Of course. Always," I said.

5

The boombox on the nightstand between our beds fired up at the push of a button. Before his voice was drowned out, Officer John said something ending with *good little man*. For reasons I couldn't figure, it choked me up. But the piano and lyrics of "Home, Sweet, Home" started up, and my thoughts drew away. It was Mitch's tape, though he wouldn't have minded me playing it. Mama didn't care for Mötley Crüe. Called it devil music. I didn't agree—they sounded perfectly fine to me—but I couldn't hear them talking, and she wasn't calling for me to turn it off. So, I let it play.

My pack lay on the floor against the chipped wooden legs at the foot of my bed. The school year beat it up good. Whatever tan coloring it had now looked a shade of sick. A small tear ran a couple inches near the end of the zipper at the top. Reggie had taken a black marker to the front. Drew a silly spiky-haired monster with its tongue sticking out, which some of our classmates made fun of. Earned me the nickname Spike at school from some of the guys who got their rocks off picking on smaller kids. Mitch called them dull-ards. But my friends knew not to call me that, so it didn't matter. We had our own names for one another, and it worked fine.

The pack was crammed full of papers. Most of them graded tests and homework I'd never shown Mama. With school now out, they hardly mattered anymore. I turned the pack upside down and paperwork and a few half-chewed pencils scattered across the floor like confetti. Left plenty of room for the shoe box.

Unlike my pack, the box was as good as new. Mama bought me a pair of Adidas for Christmas and I had stored the box under the bed. Mitch taught me to save the boxes. He said they were good to have around. You never knew when you were going to find the perfect toad or need to trap a spider to take outside. Or … have something else you might need to carry. This one would carry Mitch to Spook Hill. At least for a few hours. After I found the witch, she could do her magic. Then he could walk himself home and I could catch him up on everything he missed.

Then this stupid week could end, and Mama and Mitch and I could be happy again.

The Ziploc inside gave off a deep campfire scent. It fit nicely end to end, filled with black sooty ash from the fire pit at the Mall. Mama wouldn't notice the switch. Not until we were well gone anyway.

The box nestled into my pack with little is-sue. Took a bit of a tug to zip it up, though a blue corner of the box poked out of the inch-long rip. There wasn't much room otherwise, which was fine. The map would go in my back pocket. Dunk was loading his pack with snacks. Mo had juice boxes. Reggie said she was bringing camping and first aid supplies, though I told her we wouldn't need them. We only had until sunset anyway. After that, it would probably be too late.

Mitch said the witch told him the more time passes, the harder it is to bring the soul back to its body. First few days, the soul tends to stay nearby, clinging to the world it wasn't ready to be gone from. After that it starts to pull away. By the fifth day, it comes to terms with it and moves on. It had already been three days since the accident.

Zippy had been gone barely a day when the witch brought him back, and still, for a week or so after, he didn't seem right. So there wasn't a debate about it. Get there before sunset, take care of business, then back home by nightfall. End of story. I couldn't take any chances with my brother's soul moving on.

Mitch told me he drew the map to Spook Hill after he took Zippy. He said that finding his way through the woods wasn't easy, but he'd managed in a few hours. Finding the witch, however, took longer. Spook Hill only had a couple of roads, but it was a big place to cover.

The notebook that held the map was toward the back of Mitch's private writings. I didn't want to pry, so I passed all the pages without looking, until I reached the map. It tore free easy. Before I put the notebook back in the nightstand, I fished the perforated bits out from the spirals and tossed them in the small metal trash bin by my bed. Mitch always fussed about them. He liked his spirals clean. He'd be madder if he knew I left them in there. Best not to test him too much. Hopefully, he'd forgive me going in his notebook.

The route to Spook Hill was pretty easy. From the Mall, it was north along a winding trail through the woods to Highway 100, then left across the bridge over Edgewater Creek, then along the road until it reached a road at the edge of Spook Hill. Mitch drew a line that went about halfway up, leading to an *X* and the number *3702*. If we kept a good pace, we could be there by two or three. I couldn't begin to guess how long it would take once we were there, but if all went well, we'd be back before dark. Trouble would be waiting, no doubt, but Mama and the others would understand when they saw Mitch with us.

They'd be grateful. Any punishment I would get would be worth it.

Mama always checked in on me before bedtime, so I stuffed the bag and map under my bed. Only other thing I needed from home was Mitch's green Easton, and that stayed with me. If I could have carried it everywhere, I would have. Instead, I kept it in my bed. Thirty-two inches, twenty-eight ounces, a bit heavy in my hands. Most of the print worn off from all the contact he made. I didn't have my own bat. If I had, it would have been much smaller and lighter and looked as clean as the shoe box. I really loved baseball. I just really sucked at it. Mitch said I'd get better, once my body remembered it was supposed to grow.

The white tape around the grip was stained with use and sticky to the touch. Left a bit of tack on my palm when I tightened my hands around it. Mitch tried hard to teach me how to hit. He said to meet the ball out front and drive through it. Watch it all the way in. Sounded simple when he said it. Not so simple when some kid was firing a fastball at me. Take one of those in the arm or leg and it would hurt for days. No thanks. I'd rather step out of the box and take my chances with a flailing swing. Mitch never stepped out. Ever. He turned into each pitch, took it off his body, and headed to first without a word said. Next time up he'd hit it square up the middle, Make the pitcher skip to avoid taking it on his ankles.

I straightened to take a few practice cuts when Mama's voice rose over the music. Took some doing not to run straight out and see what the commotion was about. Instead, I lowered the music a touch, then crawled to the gap at the base of the door. First thing that hit me was the smell. Our carpet smelled like dirty feet bathed in mushroom soup. Despite it, I pressed my cheek down until I could see under the door.

Mama's legs went in and out of view as she paced in front of the television. Officer John responded, from somewhere near the sofa, but I couldn't see him.

"I'm not saying Mitch had anything to do with it. We all know the kid's a bad seed. Probably made the pickup days before. Mitch just happened to be there with him, so we have to include him in the investigation."

"He was a good boy, John. You had no right to run any tests."

"Rights aren't the issue, Morgan. The law is. We're trying to find the source."

"He wouldn't have—"

"I know." Officer John stepped into view, just a foot or so from Mama. "I know, Morgan. The boys know. It'll come back clean. I doubt the same for Gordon."

I couldn't see Mama's face, but I heard the sniffles. "How much?" she asked, voice breaking.

"A lot. Hidden away in the car. We'll be able to tie him to the action at school. Even if we can't, he's going away. For a long time, probably. Unless he wants to give up his source."

I drew a deep breath and almost choked on the stench. Held my hand tight against my mouth to keep the cough from giving me away. It calmed after a few seconds. Mama wasn't calling me, so I figured I was in the clear.

By the time I made it back to the floor, Officer John and his shiny boots were heading for the door, Mama right behind.

"The Boys are on it. Won't be long, I imagine. Not too many places to go. I don't expect any trouble, but I'll keep a watch out."

Mama followed him out. Storm door muffled what she said, but I knew the silence that followed meant they were either kissing or hugging. Or both. His boots hit solid on the patio steps. A car door closed, engine roared to life. My windows lit up. Then he was gone.

I leapt into the bed, music off, lights out when Mama shut the front door. I didn't want to talk. I just wanted the morning to come so I could get going. Whatever it was he'd done, jail wasn't enough for Gordon. He had to pay. If not for the accident, then for Zippy.

Tomorrow he would.

The barrel of the Easton fit snug against my chest. I wrapped myself into it.

6

I t wasn't going to happen. Nothing Mitch said or did would change that.

"My teammates are right. I'm garbage."

Gordon corralled the ball near the backstop and fired it hard at Mitch. It whizzed by me like a bumble bee. Mitch barely moved his glove. The pop of the ball hitting leather echoed across the empty field. "They have a point." Gordon leaned into the fence, lower lip extended by the chaw pressed into his gum. When he spit, half of it dribbled down his chin. "You can't hit shit."

"I can hit you." I cocked the bat.

"Ooh. Tough talk. I like it. Wanna bet, runt nuts?"

"You gonna cheat again?"

"Didn't cheat before. You made a bad bet."

Mitch cut the fight short with a whistle that rose like a shriek through his teeth. I couldn't do that either. Always wound up spitting all over myself. "No more bets. I already told you. Leave him be."

Gordon shrugged, kicked at the fence.

"You wanna quit, Mark?" Mitch slapped the ball into his mitt a few times. "That what you want?"

I didn't have an answer. Of course I wanted to quit. I sucked.

"You know how many balls I so much as touched my first year?"

"It isn't my first year. It's my third."

"Point's the same." He didn't give me time to respond. "None. Whole year. Nothing. Next year, I fouled a few off. Third year I squared pitches up. Fourth year I hit leadoff. You know why?"

I dragged my cleat through the dry clay and stared at the three-pronged lines. "Because you didn't quit?"

"Because I didn't quit. Because I hit off a tee every day. Because I learned to set my feet, watch the ball, and meet it out front. Same as you can. You want something, you have to go for it, okay? You can't just mope about what's what. Do something. So, you wanna quit, or are you going to step in the box and drive this pitch back at me?"

Gordon gave a snicker of a laugh. It set my teeth to grinding. My grip tightened on the handle of the bat. The Easton was too heavy for me, heavier still after so many swings, but I stepped back in the box, locked my arms, choked up on the bat and set it at an angle over my shoulder. A simple nod to Mitch and he set to throw.

The moment the pitch left his hand I felt my front foot bail. Still, I saw the ball all the way in and dropped the bat head to meet it. My weight was off. I knew I was reaching. But somehow the bat found the ball. It hugged the ground past first base like a cue shot, into right field. The vibration running through the aluminum bat stung my hands, and I let it fly halfway through my swing. It clunked on the hard infield dirt and rattled into a roll a few feet off.

"Double down the line!" Mitch threw his glove in the air, raced to me, gave me a high five. My hand was too numb to feel his hand hit mine, but the sound was solid enough to bring a smile. The ball came to a stop halfway into the outfield, almost buried in the tall grass. I'd hit it pretty good. Maybe he was right. With a little more practice, I could learn to hit it square.

Gordon strolled by, hands in his pockets, stopped a few feet along the foul line like he was measuring it. "First base, unassisted. Out."

"Dammit. Would you just—" Mitch took me by the shoulders after I picked up the bat, leading me past. "No way anyone's fielding that. It was a bullet. A rocket shot. Tony Gwynn couldn't have hit it harder. I told you there's a Hall of Fame bat in you. Thirteen next month, and once you hit your growth spurt, you'll have the tools to be a pro. Good job, little Murph." He knocked me a step forward with a solid pat to the back. I couldn't decide what made me happier, the hit, or Mitch's joy in it.

"Just keep that foot out of the bucket. Plant it. Don't raise it for nothing. Like you're in concrete. Shoulders square. Meet the ball out front and drive through it." He mimicked a swing. Even without a bat it looked perfect.

"Take a few dozen pitches in the ass and you won't be so afraid of getting hit. Be glad to help you out with that."

Mitch sighed and rolled his head skyward. "God-damn, Gordon. You're a pain in the ass, you know?"

"That's the last thing my daddy said to me before they locked him up."

"Yeah, well, I'm saying it now. Douche."

"Prick."

If I hadn't known them both so long, I'd have thought they were about to come to blows. But they laughed it off, like it was some kind of game. Gordon charged into the outfield, circled the ball and picked it up, bounced it in his left hand. He was halfway to tossing it to the backstop when a white blur streaked along the fence, stopped in line with him.

"Holy mother ball sucker. Everyone freeze."

I'd seen the albino rabbit dozens of times before. A fluffy blanket of snowy white and two ruby red eyes. Cute as all get out. It lived in the woods beyond the outfield fence, but snuck inside where the fencing was loose at the ground. I complete-ly let a ball bounce past me during a game once because I was too busy watching it run about. I named it Zippy. When it got to running, I'd never seen anything so fast.

"Gordon, don't do it."

It took me a second to figure out what Mitch meant. It was a second too long. Gordon turned to Zippy, arm back, ball gripped tight. It happened in a blur. A horrible, gut-wrenching blur. The ball let free, whistling as it cut through the air. The sick thud of contact. The spastic hops of Zippy as he bound a few steps, fell, flailed about. The still white form shaded in red. Gordon's celebratory hoot.

"Nailed it!"

I couldn't think. Through a shade of fury, I just reacted. Gordon didn't see me coming. Mitch screamed at me to stop, tried to reach for the bat, but it was too late. By the time Gordon turned, I was already swinging. Purest swing I'd ever taken. Foot planted, shoulders square, bat cutting through the zone. Perfect. Left only enough time for Gordon to turn away, like a hitter when a pitch is bearing down on them. The barrel met the back of his left shoulder. Something cracked. He screamed and dropped. Mitch shot between us before Gordon could stand, the Easton pried from my grip. He shoved me to the ground, away from Gordon.

Gordon's eyes flashed wild, breath fast and heavy through his nostrils. His left arm dangled loose. The merest effort to raise it elicited a full-on scream. "That's my pitching arm, you little shit! You're dead!"

It's like he didn't even notice Mitch there, bat hoisted and ready.

"Back off, cuz. We're not doing this today." Mitch matched each step Gordon took, turned so he was lined up as if he were in the batter's box waiting for the pitch. "I'm serious. Just go home. Go on. Tell your mom you fell making a catch in the outfield, fell off the fence, tripped on a bat. Whatever you have to say."

"He hit me with the goddamn bat! I think my shoulder's broke!"

Mitch nodded. "Tell her that then, if you want to answer to why he did it."

For a moment he acted like he would, then spit his tobacco out at Mitch's shoes. Aunt Dawn had a vicious temper. I'd seen it in person. I'd seen the bruises he wore from it. Gordon rounded toward the infield, Mitch staying with him, keeping between us. After one more good stare, Gordon headed off, cussing the whole way.

Zippy wasn't moving. His fur ruffled in the breeze, but he couldn't feel it. It was only then that it hit me what it meant. That Zippy was dead. That he'd never run again. The tears came hard and heavy. I couldn't have stopped them if I wanted. Mitch knelt, pulled me in, but didn't say a word. He just let me cry, let me snot all over his shirt, let me shake until the worst of it passed.

"He killed him." I tried to wipe my nose with my sleeve, but it only spread it around more. "Why did he do that?"

Mitch looked away. At Zippy. "I don't know, buddy. People do stupid things. Gordon just does more of them more often."

"I don't want him to be dead."

"I don't either," he says. "But sometimes …"

I wasn't sure if he couldn't finish the thought or if there wasn't anything else to add. I didn't care. I couldn't get the sound of the ball hitting Zippy out of my head. "It's wrong. He didn't do anything. Gordon's the one who should be—"

"Don't you dare finish that!" Mitch set me at arm's length, eyes hard on mine. I didn't say anything back, much as I wanted to. "Don't be what you hate. Ever. Be better than it. Now, go get the shoe box out of my bat bag. I'll put him in there. Then ... then I'll take care of it."

"Will you bury him in the yard? Please?"

Mitch eyed Zippy. Held it a moment. "Nah. I have a better idea."

7

Another minute flipped by. 8:45. The red numbers seemed to burn hotter. Like they were mad at me for still sitting on the floor. Two hours had passed, and I hadn't moved. If the bed wasn't at my back, I'd have probably dropped flat on the floor, curled up with my pack and bat, and never moved again. I needed to get up, but the fear wouldn't let me.

What if Mama had the box?

What if I couldn't find what I needed at the Junkyard?

What if I made it to the witch and she couldn't ...

She could. She had to.

My arms trembled.

I was supposed to be gone already. The walk to the Junkyard would take thirty minutes. No way I could avoid being late now. If my friends didn't wait, I'd be on my own. I couldn't do this alone. And if I waited much longer, there wouldn't be time to do it at all. It'd take a while to find Gordon's car, then it was at least another twenty minutes through the woods to the Mall. Then, from there, we had to find the trail. We'd be pushing dark getting back as it was. Any later and we had bigger problems. Trying to get through the woods at night would be impossible, even with Mitch leading the way.

A sting ran deep into my chest. The corner of the box peeking out of the rip in my pack jabbed into my collar bone. My arms wrapped tight around the pack like it was the only thing keeping me alive. I didn't know how long the box had been like that, but the sting didn't go away when I lowered the pack. In fact, it spread until my entire body ached.

"Get up, Mark. Get up and go. Now. You have to. Mitch needs you."

Mama's door was always open unless she was out of her room. I just needed to sneak in, switch the ashes, then sneak out and go. That's all. If she woke, I only had to be faster than her. She'd forgive me later. I didn't want it to go like that, but there was no other way.

Dishes clinked.

My heart beat so hard I thought it might bust through.

Mama was up.

I'd waited too long.

She couldn't be up. That wasn't the plan.

I bounded to my feet as if my legs hadn't refused to budge for the past two hours. The door stuck in the frame. In the summer months, the humidity made the wood swell. Took my shoulder to knock it loose, setting it to pop and rattle as it swayed outward, into the wall. From the sink, Mama gave me a tired smile.

"Morning, baby. You hungry? I was just about to make some eggs."

I wasn't and I'd never hated the thought of eggs so much in my life.

"No, ma'am." My stomach hurt. I was pretty sure I'd never be hungry again.

Her bedroom door was shut. She'd already showered and looked presentable. On Saturdays, she was always in her blue sleeping gown until late morning. She showered while I watched cartoons. It was all wrong. Mitch was waiting. I couldn't go tomorrow. This was the fourth day. There wouldn't be a fifth. Mitch would be gone.

"Cereal?"

Took me a second, but I shook my head. Words weren't coming.

"Pancakes?"

With Mama up and about and already showered, I didn't have any chance at all.

"You need to eat something, Markie. It's been a tough week." She lowered to me, her hands on my shoulders, and kissed my forehead. "I know I haven't given you much since … Well, I know. I've been … It's been hard. Let me make it up to you. Whatever you want for breakfast. Then we'll spend the day together, okay? Just you and me. We could go watch that *Indiana Jones* movie you wanted to see."

Her eyes glistened. I looked away, but the only place I could think to look was her door. When she noticed, the slim line of her smile dropped.

"Don't be mad. We can talk about it. It'll just be the two of us."

Now there were tears. She pulled back, arms folded.

"I'm not mad." Spending the day with Mama sounded nice, though I'd already watched the movie with my friends. Mitch got most of the attention. Usually, she'd ask him what he wanted to eat on Saturday. He was older. He got to choose. Mitch always said the same thing, even if she only gave in every once in a while. It was the best answer I could think of, and I could only hope she'd bite. "Donuts!"

When her smile returned, I saw Mitch. I'd never really noticed how much his trouble-making grin matched Mama's. "Donuts? We haven't had donuts in a while, have we? I like it! We could sit around for your cartoons, eat donuts, then go watch the movie. How's that sound?"

It sounded perfect. Like something I'd very much like to do. If I could. I nodded. It felt less like a lie that way. Not that I felt better about it. The sting in my chest pressed again like a pinecone trying to worm its way to my stomach.

Mama clapped her hands and hopped into action. "Give me a few minutes and we'll head out. We can talk on the way."

"Head out? You want me to go with you?" If I left with her, that'd be the end of that. "Can I stay here?"

"You don't want to go with me?" It was like watching all the happy melt away. Every part of her body seemed to let go at once. My shoes were all I could stand to look at.

"I—" Answers drifted around my head like dandelion seeds on the breeze. "Please? Can I stay here? I just, I really don't feel like being out. I want to be here. With Mitch."

Mama had this way of looking at me sometimes. Eyes cut, teeth clamped on the bottom of her lip. Like she was sorting through my head to see all my devilish plans. She didn't ask, but I still worried she had it all figured out. I pushed back against the desire to confess to everything. Even the things I hadn't done.

"All right. It's your day. Stay here." Her bedroom door didn't open much. She squeezed through, into the darkness, then closed it. Sounded like she was talking to herself a moment, then it got quiet.

Took a few minutes for her to return. I watched every second on the clock above the television. When Mama wedged her way out of her room, she almost clipped her heel shutting the door so fast. After a kiss on my head, she jingled her keys. "Back in about fifteen minutes. I'll get a mix. Sure you don't want to come with me?"

"Sure, Mama."

"Just stay—" Whatever she wanted to say didn't make it out. She looked me over, smiled a smile that was somehow sad at the same time. "You're growing up so fast." Then she was gone, eyes welled with tears.

As soon as the car cranked, I jumped to my feet. The sting in my chest left with her. At a distance from the diamond-shaped window high on the front door, I watched her reach the end of the long muddy drive. When she turned right, I sprinted to my room.

I'd checked the pack already, but I did it again anyway. Patted the back pocket of my jeans to confirm I had the map. Not that a shoe box of ashes or a folded map were going anywhere on their own. I just couldn't help myself. Once I left, that was it. I couldn't return without Mitch. In the living room, I set the Easton by the door and wiggled the box halfway out, until the lid opened enough for me to fish out the baggie. The ashes felt heavier than before. Now that I looked at them in daylight, I could see visible bits of charred twig poking into the plastic. I should have been more careful. If Mama looked too close, she'd know in a flash that they weren't right.

Nothing I could do about it.

There wasn't a breath deep enough to make me feel at peace.

Maybe when I was on my way, I'd feel better.

Maybe when I was back with Mitch, Mama would forgive me.

Even though she was gone, I took her bedroom door easy. Like she'd sense anything more and turn the car around. Silly though I knew it was, sometimes I'd swear she had a crystal ball. She came to school during lunch once. Said she sensed I'd caused a scene in class. Just an hour before I'd gotten into it with Mr. Vance over math problems. He gave me detention. Mama gave me worse.

The shades were drawn. Bedroom was mostly dark, but with enough light to see the white box on the dresser. I let loose a sigh of relief. Just a quick switch and I'd be gone and on my way. Maybe Mama would look at them today, maybe she wouldn't. I'd have a head start no matter.

The box wasn't anything extraordinary. White oak, trimmed in swirls of gold. Gold latch on the front, small knob to lock it shut. Looked more like one of Mama's jewelry boxes than, well, than what it was. Picking it open wasn't easy. The tiny knob slotted tight. When I finally got it turned and released the latch, the lid was lighter than expected. It clapped against the dresser like a gunshot, which gave me as much a start as the bag within.

For a moment, I froze, staring at it. A charred silver medallion tied the top of a clear baggie. My bag—a plain ole zip top that looked nothing like the thick-walled plastic bag in the box—didn't have a medallion. I wasn't even sure why it was there. The slightest scent of soot tickled my nose. The bag was much smaller than I'd expected. Much too small for Mitch. It should have been bigger. Mine was almost twice the size.

It's not Mitch. That can't be Mitch. There's not enough in there.

Someone groaned.

That's when I noticed the belt and holstered gun at the end of the dresser.

"Mark?"

I didn't turn. I didn't need to. I could see him in the mirror atop the dresser. I turned my gaze back to the box, like I'd peeked in on something I shouldn't have seen.

Officer John rustled the sheets aside. The bed creaked when he sat up. He made a noise like a yawn, though it could as easily have been a gasp. I had no idea what to do, but as if I was one of his suspects, my hands rose. If he didn't see the bag before, he would now.

"Turn around, Mark."

I had a vision of Mama coming home to find me in handcuffs, bawling and stuffed in the back of Officer John's car. Prison would be better than what she'd do to me.

But whatever Mama would do wouldn't be worse than failing Mitch.

Mama had never had a man over before. It'd just been the three of us forever. Didn't even know I had a daddy until I learned that he ran off to have another family elsewhere before I was born. I didn't want to see Officer John in her bed, but I couldn't let him stop me neither. The bag in the box was there for the taking, wide white sticker on the plastic blaring "Mitchell Murphy" at me. As fast as I could, I swapped out the baggie of firepit ash for the bag in the box. I knew instantly that Mama wouldn't be fooled. My bag didn't fit in the box well enough to close the lid, and the bag I held didn't feel like ash at all. Some of the bits within were sharp against my palms, like ground pebbles.

Like ground bone.

When I gave it a squeeze, it didn't give the same as my bag. I pinched the medallion between my fingers, looking for some sign I had it all wrong. That this wasn't Mitch. But the inscription bore his name. Black soot marked my fingers. I'd printed the lid of the box with sooty fingerprints.

Something in my throat twitched and I nearly threw up.

"Mark?"

Once the lid to the white box was as shut as it'd get, I turned to Officer John, bag clutched to my chest.

A white tank top covered some of his hairy chest, slacks draped over the wooden chair by the wall, shoes on the floor at the foot of the bed. I knew I could get all the head start I needed. Couldn't imagine he'd chase me outside in his briefs and bare feet.

"Put the bag back, Mark."

I slid a step toward the door. "I have to go. Tell Mama it'll be all right. We'll be back later."

"What do you mean? What are you doing?"

The sheets shifted aside. A bit of hairy leg draped over the edge of the bed, challenging me. Not wanting to wait until he completely stood, I took off. The trailer floor shook as he landed hard, calling my name, but I got to my pack in a flash. By the time he reached the bedroom door, trousers half on in a one-legged dance, Mitch's ashes were in the shoe box, pack zipped, bat in hand.

"Whatever you're doing, think about your mom. She doesn't need this." He nearly tripped trying to get his second leg in but caught himself on the doorframe.

"She needs Mitch. So do I." And I ran.

"Needs Mitch? Mark, your brother—" Officer John's voice cut short as the storm door clapped shut. His patrol car was there, right out front of my bedroom window. If I had looked at all, I'd have seen it. Better I didn't. I wouldn't have chanced going in the room.

Sky was still grey, but the rain had finally stopped. Mosquitos were out in full force, air thick and swampy. The yard and drive were nothing but puddles. Much more and we'd have been the start of a new pond. I did my best not to slosh, but the faster I ran, the more impossible it became. Water seeped through the legs of my jeans. My sneakers were coated in mud and heavy as tires.

I didn't look back until I reached the end of the long drive, and only then because I heard the siren of the patrol car yelp. Officer John shouted something I couldn't make out, half in the car, uniform shirt unbuttoned. The Junkyard was to the right, straight down Moody Road into downtown Hogan, but I wouldn't get far with Officer John trailing me. Only choice was to cut straight across Moody, through the Herberts' lot, into the woods behind their house, until I reached the train tracks. They ran along the same path as Moody, but with no cross street until Silver Lake Drive in town. The Junkyard was on the other side of the Square.

Another blast of the siren gave me a jolt as I crossed the road, but there was no way I was looking back.

I hit the tracks at full speed and didn't slow down, no matter how much it hurt, no matter how hard it was to breathe. If I kept at a run, I could cut some time. Hopefully, my friends would wait for me.

By the time I neared the break in the trees just outside of downtown, my legs were screaming for rest. I didn't want to chance coming out in the open, so I ducked back into the woods the rest of the way.

At the clearing near the Square, I saw the swirling lights and knew I was in for it.

8

The city of Hogan wasn't much more than a sneeze in the center of Boiling County. Most of the few restaurants and odds-and-ends stores we had lined a roundabout that circled the Boling County courthouse, which was easily the most impressive building in town, if not the county. It was white and gleaming, lined in columns at the entrance, a steepled roof topped with a golden statue of Lady Justice, and I'd spent countless hours sprawled on the grassy lawn with Reggie, Mo, and Dunk, watching people meander in and out, wondering what cases were happening inside.

Only other places of business were on the opposite end of Moody Road, where Mama had gone to buy donuts. She'd be home now. In a state because of what I'd done. I tried not to think about it too hard. It made my chest ache.

The railroad tracks I'd followed emerged from the woods about fifty yards from downtown, where they crossed Silver Lake Drive. Town folk called the crossing guard the Shaking Fist. Probably because the signal sounded like an old man complaining every time a train cut by. The faded red-and-white arms always bounced off the road when they dropped, the signal hollow and dull like a cracked bell. Even when the train cleared and the arms went back up, it clanked a bit longer, like it still had things to say no matter if traffic could move again or not.

Just beyond the tracks, facing up Silver Lake, sat a squad car, off the road in the grass, lights twirling. It wasn't Officer John. This guy was much younger. He drummed away at the wheel, pausing long enough to wave when a car passed. Then he'd take a casual look down the tracks and drum some more.

"He called for backup?"

With nothing but open space from the woods to the short alley between the back walls of businesses, my choices were slim: either I took the chance of being seen running to the alley or I cut back through the woods, all the way over to Moody. But getting through the thick brambles and brush in this part of the woods would cost me time I didn't have to lose. From where I stood, the path to the courthouse was shorter. A direct line. If I could get to the alley and across downtown, I'd be home free to the Junkyard.

I gave the strap of my pack a tug, hoisted it higher on my shoulder, bat gripped tight. Then I waited. After a few moments, another car crawled up Silver Lake toward the tracks, slowing to gawk at the officer in his car. As soon as his head turned, hand raised to wave, I took off.

From a glass-half-full perspective, it seemed like a good plan. Head down, pack bouncing against my back, I almost smiled at my cleverness. But halfway, I realized I hadn't measured the water in the glass at all. If Officer John wanted backup to watch for me, of course he wouldn't just cover one side of town. Open and exposed in the clearing between the tracks and businesses, I could see that the young officer wasn't alone. Parked in the grass to my left off Moody, in clear view, another set of lights twirled my nerves into a bundle. Unlike the younger officer, this one leaned against the grill of his car, arms crossed, watchful eyes hidden underneath the darkest of sunglasses. The second he saw me, his posture changed. Like an Olympic runner triggered by the starting gun, he reached a dead sprint in a matter of steps. My lead evaporated in a hurry. Fueled by his speed, I found another gear, but getting to the other side of the roundabout free of followers seemed less and less likely.

A boom of voice cut across the clearing, drawing the younger officer quickly out of his car. "... he's on foot from the tracks ..."

As the officer behind narrowed the gap, the younger one cut straight down Silver Lake toward the courthouse to head me off. Caught trying to judge my lead as I reached the alley, I completely looked past the trash bins lining the wall near the exit and clipped one with the Easton. It rattled to the ground in a clatter of metal, the bat knocked clean out of my hand. By the time I recovered it, the officer from Moody was nearly on me. No way I'd make it now.

But I couldn't stop. I couldn't quit. Getting Mitch back was more important than any trouble I'd be in. If I had to swing my way out of it with the Easton, I'd do it.

Early morning on a Saturday left downtown quiet. Most of the businesses didn't even open until ten. The roundabout was clear, no folks walking anywhere I could see. Made it easier to navigate, but meant I was that much easier to follow. To my right, the young officer cleared the businesses at a full run. Gun drawn, arms pumping stiffly at his side, he moved at an angle toward the front of the courthouse, forcing me the longer way around the back of the building.

A gun?

I about peed myself.

All this because I took Mitch's ashes?

The driveway to the Junkyard was on past the courthouse, a quarter of a mile down from where Moody picked up again out of the roundabout. The gang would hopefully still be in the woods near the entrance, waiting for me. Of course, if the officers followed me into the woods, we'd never make it into the Junkyard. If I ran further and hit the woods past the Junkyard, then tried to trail back, it'd cost more time.

But it beat losing the only chance I had to get what I needed.

Maybe I could lose them in the woods past the Junkyard, then circle back when they cleared out.

With no other choice, I lowered my head, tightened my hands around the straps of my pack to keep it from bouncing side to side, and ran as fast as I could.

When I was barely past the courthouse, the officers were twenty yards at the most behind. By the time I reached the drive to the Junkyard, they'd catch me. Whatever burst of speed I had found began to fade as my leg muscles burned. I could barely breathe. My feet felt numb, my balance off as everything in me screamed for it all to stop.

"Cut him off on that side!"

"Wait! Chet, hold up!"

By the time I crossed the roundabout on my way toward the other end of Moody, they had slowed to a stop. Much though I wanted to follow their lead and take a moment to rest, I needed to take advantage of the break. When I finally turned, the younger officer had holstered his gun, a long thin finger pointed my way. The other barked a word loud enough for all the world to hear—one of those words Mama would have grounded me for saying—wiped his brow, then clicked the radio mic. Then they just stood there, watching me run off into the woods.

They had to know where I was going. That's why they stopped. Which meant Officer John would too. That was probably why they called it in. He'd be on his way. I wanted to hate him for putting this much into pursuing me, but he was doing right by Mama. Despite what it meant for me, it was at least good to know that much.

But it didn't matter what Officer John wanted. I couldn't let him stop me. I'd just have to be quick about finding the wrecked car, grab what I needed, and move on.

The driveway to the Junkyard lay past another line of businesses along Moody, a big billboard-sized sign planted by the road, hand-painted scrawl faded by the sun. The property sat back in the woods, surrounded by a chain-link fence covered in green windscreen, topped by curls of barbed wire.

The woods smelled like a bog, all wet soil and greenery. Bugs swarmed thick in the air, clusters of gnats following me like they'd never tasted sweat so sweet. The ground swallowed my steps, gave a gross sticky sound like smacking on cereal. In between, a conversation carried through the trees that once again drew me to a stop.

In front of the Junkyard office, just past a squad car parked in the gravel drive leading to the open swing gate, another officer stood in conversation with Tank McGee. Tank filled most of the opening, the officer dwarfish by comparison. Arms crossed over a grungy Metallica t-shirt stretched tight across his large gut, Tank looked like he was defying anyone to pass. The officer certainly wasn't trying. He stood about ten feet back, hands deep in his pockets.

I was so focused on them both that I didn't see Dunk move from behind a tree to my left. I about jumped out of my skin when he touched my shoulder.

Dunk shushed me like I didn't know to be quiet. Mo and Reggie wandered into view, looking more like the friends I'd known for years, less like the costumed versions I'd seen the day before at church—Mo in his treasured *True Blue* tour shirt and jeans and Reggie's hair back in pigtails underneath a grimy Braves cap, blue denim overalls over a short-sleeved shirt. Their packs were stuffed, filled with everything they promised to bring.

Mo tapped his watch with a fingernail. The digital 9:23 blinked out a second, then fluttered a bit before it reappeared. The watch had been dying a while now, ever since he forgot to take it off when we splashed around in the ankle-deep water of Edgewater Creek a month before, but he refused to tell his parents. It had been a present just before that on his thirteenth birthday, after all, and his family preached hard about respecting gifts given.

"I know," I whispered. Then pointed toward the fence running away from the entrance and through the woods. "Over there."

The canopy of trees offered more than enough coverage to keep us hidden. Tank's voice carried over any sound we made, and the officer wasn't giving much notice to anything else. Once clear of the entrance, out of sight, we cut to the fence. The muddy path running alongside to the back would be easier to walk, with fewer leaves and branches crunching at our feet.

It was also easier to hear.

"This is the only way. And he ain't gettin' in." Tank spat as if it were punctuation. Mama had known him since grade school. She said he did that even back then. "Every bit of fence is blocked by cars. Has been for years. Damn kids were in here all the time before. Ain't moving them to get through. Ain't climbing over top. Ain't passing me. Ain't getting in."

"Maybe I should check the lot? Just in case?"

"Told your bossman already, he's the only one getting past me. Nobody else. Sure as hell ain't no kid getting in. Hear me?"

"Yeah, I hear you, Tank."

Silence slipped in, broken by the call of the radio. "What's your 20, Brice?"

"Speak of the devil," said Brice, a simple laugh that Tank didn't return.

Officer John. It was suddenly hard to swallow. "At the Junkyard, over."

A sharp whine of static filled the air. "Roger that. Perimeter secure?"

Tank spat. Enough said.

"Ten-four. All clear. He hasn't been here. Tank's … Well, he isn't getting in here."

Silence. Static.

"Keep an eye on Moody. Last report had him in the vicinity heading your way. I'll be there shortly."

"Roger that."

I didn't wait for anything else. We couldn't be anywhere near the Junkyard when Officer John arrived. I led my friends along the fence, around a right turn, and toward the back center of the lot. The woods thickened, crowded with pines and overgrowth. The path along the fence was difficult but worn enough by the scores of other kids before us to make it passable.

"Dudes, I packed Uno, in case anyone wants to get destroyed." When we didn't respond, Dunk snorted. "Totally get it. I'm the Uno King."

"You're a cheat is what you are," snapped Mo. "Nobody gets four Draw Four wild cards in one hand. Nobody."

"Come on now," said Dunk, a short laugh after. "Lady Luck was on my side. Just because you all couldn't beat me—"

"What about that game of Battleship, where every shot you took somehow hit our ships?" Reggie's head cocked to the side, eyes wide, way more threat in her face than her words.

Mo jabbed the air with a finger. "Or the game of Stratego where you never hit a bomb and always found our flags?"

Dunk stood in place, mouth open, shoulders slumped. "It's luck, I tell ya! I'd never cheat any of you! What about … What about …." He snapped his fingers, a loud crack that shot through the trees. "Monopoly! That game of Monopoly we played last summer. Took weeks to finish and I didn't win. I went bankrupt in the second week!"

We came to a stop several feet ahead of Dunk, exchanged a few nods. "Fair point," I said to Mo and Reggie. "Spent half his time in jail, didn't he? Only had houses on Baltic and Mediterranean.

Too broke to afford anything else, especially being that he was Mo's best tenant on Park Place."

Mo planted his chin in a hand, eyeing Dunk suspiciously. "And he *was* the thimble. No true gamer ever picks the thimble."

Reggie nodded. "Dog, all the way."

"Battleship," I said, perhaps a bit quicker and more excited about it than I should have been.

"Hat," said Mo. "Classic. Dignified."

Dunk nodded along, his smile widening with each reply. "Exactly! I don't even know how I'd have managed to cheat! I'm a total 'tard! I'm not even smart enough to know how to cheat myself! I swear!"

"Hm. A valid point." Mo flipped a hand in the air. "Not guilty by reason of stupidity, I suppose. Case dismissed."

Satisfied, we trudged on, nearing the halfway mark of the back fence.

"Where are we going?" Reggie was so close it sounded like she stood on my back.

"A little further."

"Tank said it's all blocked."

"It is. Sort of." I used the Easton to point at a single flap of green windscreen dangling free ahead, chain link behind cut through and folded outward. Against the gap the back end of a rusty school bus pressed into the fence, bumper to the top of the door visible. The window above the word *Stop* was busted free. A once-white towel draped over the base of the window frame, moldy and rotten from rain and time. "Kids have been sneaking in this way for a while. Cleared out all the glass. Just have to climb through."

Dunk leaned into the bumper with all his weight. The bus bobbed. "If the bus is a rockin'."

"Ew. Gross, Dunk. Don't be a Neanderthal." Despite Mo's curled lip, he looked in the lower window as if a show was about to start. We all did.

"What? You never wanted to make out with a girl in the back of a busted-up bus in a junkyard?"

Mo planted a hand to his hip, perfect angle of his thin arm looking like a bent hanger. "I can absolutely guarantee that thought never crossed my mind."

"I have. Every day. Lindy Ratcliff. Prettiest thing on the planet. 'Course, anywhere with her would be fine by me." Dunk raised his bushy eyebrows, then made like he was kissing Lindy. It involved a lot of gross licking sounds I'd never soon forget.

Mo turned away, face a sheet of disgust. "That's so barbaric. Make it stop, Murph."

Reggie beat me to it. Slugged Dunk solid in the arm in a way only she could. She knew all our weak spots. It gave a meaty *thud*. "Can it. And if you call that kissing, you'll never get a girlfriend that isn't furry and walks on four legs."

After a rub of his arm, Dunk shrugged. "You keep punching like that, you'll never need a boyfriend."

"I don't need one now."

"Point made."

"We have to go." I jumped onto the bumper before they could continue cutting into one another. With my foot on the rim of the lower window, I could get a firm grip on the top window. The slick nastiness of the towel was disgusting. I recoiled at first; but there was no other way in. The window was plenty big enough, but it would take a pull to get through. "Dunk, you should probably stay here."

"Why, because I'm fat? You think I can't climb up through there?"

"No, it's just—" The door was cracked open an inch or two. But no way the gap in the fence was wide enough. Edges of the door were into the chain link as far as they could go. Only way in was through the window. "Yeah. Sorry."

I didn't want to look at Dunk. It felt horrible saying it. But he just nodded along like it had been his idea.

"Totally, dude. No way I'm getting through there without being all Pooh stuck in the hole to Rabbit's house. And no honey for the effort. Good call. I'll wait over there, past the shrubs. There's more ground to sit on. Leave your packs with me."

Mo and Reggie passed theirs off without making eye contact. I dropped mine into the back row of seats with the Easton, no intention of being apart from Mitch. No matter if Dunk agreed to stay behind, the urge to apologize for suggesting it bubbled up like vomit. Dunk had always been on the heavy side, but it was just one of those things we never brought up.

I looked down at them from my perch on the bumper. It was odd to stand taller than anyone. Any other time, I was looking up. Even to Reggie. "If someone sees us, split up and meet at the Mall. The trail's further on from there."

Mo let loose a throaty *Hm*. All casual and innocent like it was nothing.

But I'd heard it before. It was definitely *something*. Sounded a lot like his mother when he did it. Nothing to do but let him say what he had to say. His voice got all pitchy and impossible to take if he felt like he was being ignored.

"What?"

Like clockwork, he got this look of shock. Eyes wide, eyelids fluttering. Fingertips of one hand to the base of his throat like he was shocked to be called upon. Then his chin went up a bit and he smiled wide. Teeth crazy white and gleaming. I swear he must have visited the dentist weekly, or something. "*Moi*? Oh, nothing at all. I'm sure this will all go splendidly. I'm as confident as Marie Antoinette at the guillotine."

"I—" Dunk and Reggie shrugged when I looked to them for help. Mo was smarter than any kid I knew. And he didn't hesitate to show it. "Is that good?"

One eyebrow went up. Meant I'd swung and missed again. And it was the only reply I'd get. So, I let it go and worked my way through the window. Took far more effort than I thought it would. Mitch said I needed to lift weights. Maybe he was right. I must have looked like a flailing worm on the end of a hook trying to climb my way through.

Reggie swatted at a foot that got too close. "You sure we can get through the front?"

"Yeah." My ribs pressed into the frame and it came out more like a grunt. "Gordon says the door still opens."

"What?" Reggie's fingers buried into my calf so tight she almost pulled me out of the window. "You can't! He could be in there."

"Who?"

"Gordon! They're looking for him! That officer out there said so to Tank. Someone saw him around town. They think he's headed here."

No matter how much I pulled, I couldn't break free of Reggie's grip. Mitch was being nice. I must have been the weakest boy on the planet. "They're after him? I thought they were chasing me. Because of the ashes."

"Did your mother call them?" Mo paused at the foot of the bumper, arms wide like he was going to catch me if I fell. Not a chance. He was an inch taller than me and at least as bony-armed.

"No. Officer John saw me—" I stopped too late.

"Ooh, la la!" Dunk clicked the inside of his cheek and winked far too many times. "They finally did the deed, huh?"

"Cut it out, Duncan!" Reggie let go to land another punch to Dunk's shoulder. A solid dense sound that reminded me too much of Zippy and the ball. Free of Reggie's death grip, but with way more effort than I'd have liked, I managed my way through the window. Already up on the bumper, Reggie snaked through as easy as taking a step.

That didn't make me feel less weak at all. She must have caught my expression, because she gave me a *nah nah* kinda smile and head wobble.

"You really are a Neanderthal." Mo didn't even start the climb until Reggie and I had him by the hands. Getting him past the towel without a squeal was the hard part.

9

The interior of the bus was a mess. Rust and mossy green coated the entire shell. Deep cuts ran through the vinyl of most seats, some torn completely free, rusted springs visible, bits of shredded foam all over the floor. The few surviving seats were in a small group toward the front. Empty beer cans and cigarette butts littered the floor and aisle. I kicked a can out of the way, exposing a crumpled-up condom. Reggie covered her mouth like she was going to vomit. Couldn't blame her.

"Total gross out," I offered, rolling another nearby can back over it with my foot.

Ivy wound through busted-out windows, covered the glass of the rest. The roof along the door side bent at an unpleasant angle. The driver's seat looked in good condition, but where the wheel should have been there was just a metallic plate. The chirping song of birds drifted through the open area where the windshield once was.

First pull of the lever opened the door fine, but it screeched long and loud enough it seemed the whole world would hear it. The three of us dropped like our knees gave out. A breeze cut through the bus, but all was silent beyond. After a careful check through the open windshield, we filed out. No matter the situation, walking off the bus felt like any other day at my stop from school. Only instead of home, there was a maze of trashed cars and trucks. Some older than us. Some that clearly didn't get much driving before getting wrecked beyond repair.

From the outside, the bus looked even worse. Like it rolled and tore off half the front with it. I didn't know what had happened or when, but hopefully no kids had been on board when it did.

To either side of the bus, cars piled two and three high against the fence. The ivy had taken over most, leaving nothing but pillows of leafy green strands in the shape of cars. Along the line, a few young oaks had pushed their way through frames. They wound and stretched through any opening they could find. Like nature was playing Twister with the remains.

"Hurry up, okay?"

Dunk's voice rose from somewhere behind the piles. I couldn't tell exactly where. A quick thumbs up sent him off into the brush. He wasn't quiet about it.

In either direction, an aisle wide enough to drive through curled around and out of sight. The interior cars were all parked like we'd arrived at the lot of the Winn-Dixie from Hell, spaced evenly, every bit of empty space thick with weed and grass. The cars might have been drivable once upon a time; now they were all smashed metal and glass that unsettled my stomach. The sight of it drove home what it was I was here to look for. A realization that tore through my thoughts with visions of what I'd find. Made me that much more relieved my friends were with me.

"There are a lot of cars here," said Reggie. "We should split up. We'll find it faster."

"No. Stick together." No way I wanted to find the car alone. "To the right. A few of those at the end look like they might not have been here as long. Maybe Tank keeps newer vehicles together closer to the gate."

"But—"

"Remember what it looks like, right?"

Reggie nodded, but she never hid her disagreements well. Dark eyes cut, jaw set, nostrils flaring. Took it all just to keep her from arguing further. She got that from her dad. He wasn't much for talking, but he sure liked to argue. Loudly. I knew she was right, though I wouldn't admit to it. It'd be a lot faster to cover both sides at once. "Yeah, we remember. He made sure everyone saw him in it."

"For the longest time, I didn't even know it was a car." Mo's lip curled. "Looked more like a tacky NASCAR billboard with all those bumper stickers. So much conflicting color. So *bourgeois*."

We stared at Mo, lost in another of his big words. He'd told us often that he enjoyed reading dictionaries, in any language. He had us in the nerd department by a mile.

He rolled his eyes. "It means—never mind. Why are we here again?"

"I need something from Gordon's car. I have to take it to the witch."

Their looks cut through me. To no one's surprise, Reggie was the first to ask. "Something of Mitch's?"

I just shook my head. I didn't want to get into it. Not yet. They wouldn't like my answer.

By the time we reached a line of less destroyed cars, I'd stopped looking too close. Though most were in fair condition—older models that probably just died out—a few were smashed almost beyond recognition. Roofs battered, front ends all but gone, windshields shattered and stained a rust color that set my imagination off in a direction I'd rather it not go. Best I could do was spy rocks along the drive, kick a few and follow their path so that I could glance up every few steps.

One part of the drive hooked back to an aisle cutting through the center of the lot, another stretched along the fence fifty yards or so until it also turned off to the center. But the wrecks along the fence didn't have overgrowth and hadn't been picked clean. More space lay in between, like cars would come and go pretty often. The open gate was straight on but blocked by pick-up trucks jacked up on oversized wheels. Shiny flashes of a metallic body beneath stains of dried clay, no sign of dent or broken glass, they looked out of place with the rest. I'd heard Tank and some of his friends did some mud bogging on weekends. The trucks were probably theirs. Though approaching them took us too close to Tank for comfort, the cars along the fence seemed most promising.

Mo saw it first. About halfway to the last turn. Past a battered red Jeep with a twisted roll bar and shredded leather top. He didn't say anything. His gasp was enough. Beyond the open space after the Jeep, it was all there, hidden by nothing. It was like watching the wreck happen right then and there.

The back bumper hung from one side to the ground, seemingly held in place by a handful of those god-awful crude bumper stickers. Brake lights and the back windshield busted out. Back half of the passenger's side smashed to hell where the other car hit it. Roof crumpled down to the top of the seats all the way across from the roll. Both doors gone entirely—driver's side torn off, the passenger door cut free by the rescue team. Hood propped against the fence. Engine exposed. What remained of it rose in a pile like it got put through a blender and poured back in.

The sight of the mangled car gave my stomach a lurch it couldn't fight, my skin instantly cold and clammy, sweat beading on my forehead. I barely made it to the Jeep before I threw up. Fortunately, I hadn't eaten much since lunch the day before, making the worst of it dry heaves that burned the muscles around my ribs and made my head feel like it might explode.

Reggie moved quick behind me, saying something I couldn't hear through the pressure in my ears. I waved her off. When the heaves passed, I wiped my face on a sleeve, almost clocking myself with the handle of the Easton in the process. I had no idea I hadn't let it go.

"You all right?" Mo had my pack, handed it over, a soft pat to my shoulder.

"Yeah." I hovered near the back end of the Jeep a few seconds longer. As much to steel my nerves as to settle the last of the shakes. "Just wait here, okay? If you see Tank or Officer John heading in, let me know. And hold this." Reggie took the Easton by the barrel in both palms, gentle like she was Indiana Jones taking the Holy Grail.

They crowded tight just past the Jeep, a few steps into the open space between vehicles. Still close enough to help if I needed it, but far enough to avoid seeing anything they didn't want to re-member.

The distance to the car seemed longer with each step. I focused on the floorboard to keep from seeing the whole wreckage. To avoid think-ing about Mitch sitting in the seat. About the car getting creamed and flipped. An impossible thing to avoid. I had to move fast. Get out quick. As far away as I could. Something in my head—maybe my heart—started issuing threats. Like a volcano spewing steam before the eruption. I couldn't let that happen in front of everyone. There was no reason. No reason at all. Justice would be served, and he'd be back soon.

"Mitch will be back. Mitch will be back. Mitch will be back."

It didn't help. My whisper sounded like a shout.

One long breath freed the tightened muscles of my throat. The distance shortened. Suddenly, I was there.

Broken glass covered most of the floorboard. A deep stain ran like a dry river from the headrest to the seat. Coated the grey fabric, darkened it. In the center of the seat, a foot-long strip of duct tape had ripped down the middle, stuffing torn out. Gordon said he accidentally sliced it open when he dropped his butterfly knife while driving. The duct tape had held it together. It must have split during.

During.

During the accident.

During the accident when Mitch …

An inner earthquake built. My hands shook, the tremor rolling down my arms, all the way to my legs. Only way I'd be able to get a grip on them was to find what I came for and get on with the mission. The dashboard was mostly collapsed, but the glove compartment held fine. Mitch said Gordon kept it in there. Hopefully, nobody had taken it. It took two hands to pinch the handle in enough to open it. When it finally gave way, the hinge snapped and the compartment door fell loose, contents spilled across the floorboard and under the seat. Trying to avoid the bits of glass in the matted brown floor, I pushed things aside carefully with my fingertips. Underneath some maintenance invoices, I found the card, atop the manual, halfway under the seat.

Relief washed over me. It was there and looked as good as new.

Holding the 1978 Dale Murphy rookie card in a sealed protective sheet was like holding a piece of gold. No bends. No tears. Just the smiling face of my favorite Braves player ever. Happy to see me. Glad to be a part of my quest. I had kept it framed above my bed when it was mine. Before Gordon stole it from me with a bogus bet. He'd reminded me of it for two years straight. Nothing meant as much to him.

That's the way it had to be. The way the witch would want it.

Somewhere along the way he had punched a hole in the top of the plastic holder—fortunately not close enough to the card to expose it to any moisture—and ran a black shoelace through it. Mitch said he'd take it out of the glove compartment to hang it from the rearview mirror every time he came by. Just so I would see it.

I gave it a tug, but the lace pulled against something under the seat. Not stuck under there, just dragging whatever it was along. I nearly closed my eyes, expecting some random body part or bloody piece of clothing the whole world missed. But something metal clinked against the outer frame of the seat, and my tug popped the lace free. Though I had what I came for, the thing it dragged with it left me frozen.

The black barrel framed a narrow opening in the cylinder, a single dark eye marking me as nothing but a target. I'd seen the gun once before, but only from a distance. Gordon was showing it off to Mitch. When I got too close, Gordon buried it under his shirt. Told me to head off and keep my mouth shut. I didn't say anything, but I should have. Should have told Mama that Gordon had a gun. She'd have let Aunt Dawn know and she would have torn him a new one. Maybe she would have taken his car away.

I buried that thought, fast and furious.

I didn't really want to take it. Guns scared me from this side to the end of time. But it belonged to Gordon. As much as he seemed to love it, taking it could only help. In case the card wasn't enough. I looped the card around my neck, gun pinched between my fingers like it was the tail of a screeching rat. It could have been loaded, but I had no idea how to check. No way I'd shoot it anyway, so what did it matter? Because of the box, the pack didn't have much room. But a bit of pushing on the cardboard finally squeezed it past. My finger curled away from the trigger, but I still closed my eyes until it wedged in there. The zipper caught just past halfway. When I gave it a hard tug closed, the rip in the pack opened another inch. The box poked out a bit further, giving the gun room to slip to the bottom.

Time to go.

Pack over my shoulder I turned to Mo and Reggie.

Only they weren't alone anymore. They just didn't know it.

At the back of the Jeep, Gordon leaned into the spare tire like he was Danny Zuko, all cool against his greased lightning. The sling was gone, but the slightest movement of his left arm—tight against his body—brought a wince.

"What's up, runt nuts?"

Mo bit down on a squeal, muffled sound trapped in his mouth like he was gagged. He and Reggie backed my way as Gordon watched the entrance. When Tank's voice didn't come, he eased a few slow steps forward.

"Wouldn't expect you to come here to look at this piece of shit. Goddamn, it's trashed, isn't it? Sucks. I loved that car. Damn shame, isn't it?" I held quiet and he huffed as if my silence offended him. "Whatever. Take off already. But I want that card before you go."

Hand out. Eyebrows up. He actually expected me to do it.

I tucked the holder under my shirt. "No."

"No? Yeah, that isn't going to work." His gaze settled past me. On the car. On the passenger's seat and the mess of things on the floorboard. His cheeks paled. His eyes widened as they drifted to my pack. Something in his expression changed as fast as a light being switched off. Before I knew it, he had his butterfly knife out of his back pocket, whipping it about. I hadn't seen him this angry since I clubbed his shoulder.

"Give me the pack. Now."

I shifted it further down my back. The butt of the gun lay heavy through the fabric, pressed against my spine, taunting my bad judgment. I should have left it alone. The card would have been enough by itself. I didn't really need it. Not that giving it back now would change anything. Once Gordon tipped the edge of anger, he made no effort to maintain balance.

With surprising speed that cost him a considerable flare of pain in his shoulder, Gordon snatched Reggie by a pigtail, her head jerked back. The Easton fell from her grip, hit the ground with a dense metallic *clunk*. The whip of the blade flashed in the overcast light, came to a rest against her throat. She managed a deep breath, mouth open, ready to screech like a banshee.

"Uh-uh. Not a sound or I slice you open. Now, it's up to you, runt nuts. Give me the card and what you have in the goddamn pack or you'll be one dweeb down."

Caught in between, Mo shuffled beside me. Choked words emerged in a whimper.

I blocked Mo a bit, hoping to calm his nerves. When he got like that, it almost always closed in a pitchy squeal. One of those and none of us would get out. "Let her go and I'll give you what you want."

"I want the card and the pack. Not up for debate."

"You're not getting either."

Reggie squirmed enough to shift the blade. A thin line of red followed, like the crack of a door, a bead of blood streaking the length of her neck. It surprised Gordon enough that he drew away from her throat a couple of inches, arm draped atop her shoulder.

"Damn, Pocahontas. You in a hurry to die? That was some close shit."

"No way I'm letting a brainless punk like you kill me."

The intensity in her eyes was enough to sell me. I'd seen it before. Reggie was a good soul, no doubt, but Mama had it right. The girl had the fire of the devil in her.

"Bullshit you won't. Tell her, runt nuts."

The blade turned my way. Gordon bounced it in the air to encourage a response. It was a bad choice.

Reggie landed the full weight of a stomp on his toes, gripped his wrist in a tight clamp with both hands, twisting inward until the blade pointed at the ground. In a quick pivot, she spun ahead of his arm and buried the blade halfway into his leg. Never one to settle on enough being enough, Reggie hauled back and kicked him square in the nuts. Gordon's scream cut short in a sputtering breathless whimper.

Blood flowed from the hilt of the blade, down the leg of his jeans. Gordon toppled over, torn between cupping his crotch and grasping at the knife in his leg.

Unfortunately, the scream wasn't cut short enough.

Shouts carried over the trucks, from the entrance. Tank's barreling tone rose first, followed by the screechy static of a radio. Officer John. Calling for backup. He'd arrived.

"We'll find Dunk and meet you there!" Reggie said, dragging a stunned and unusually silent Mo away. "You get out the back and we'll head around and make our way out the front when it's clear."

I just stared at her. Partly amazed, partly flustered, every bit matching Mo's expression. Gordon rocked on the ground, battling the pain, struggling to sit up. The knife pulled free with a sickening wet sound.

"Go!" She and Mo ran off, down the center path, then quick between cars and out of sight.

I took a wide route to get past Gordon to retrieve the Easton, but with another scream leading the way, he rolled to his side to latch onto my ankle. The pain in his shoulder hit a high point as I tried to shake loose, jerking his arm back and forth. Gordon launched a few wild stabs of the bloody blade at me, digging into the wet soil, missing my leg by a few inches. A quick kick to his wrist loosened his grip, giving me time to scramble to my feet. He matched me, up in a hurry, hobbling on one leg, one hand again to his crotch, blood working its way in a hurry down to his ankle.

From the center aisle in a mad dash, Officer John shouted more orders into his radio, with a mention of Gordon by name. He'd already seen us both. I just wasn't sure who he'd follow. When he drew his gun, I backed a step, a foot landing on the handle of the Easton. The roll of the bat sent me tumbling. From my knees, I lunged for it, but Gordon beat me there. He twirled it once, baiting me.

"You want this back? Then give me what I want. Maybe then I won't bash your friends' heads in with it. See you soon, runt nuts." He hobbled toward the fence, past the Jeep, quickly out of sight.

Much though I wanted to chase after him, much though I worried I'd never see the Easton again, it made the mission that much more necessary. Once the witch did her work, I'd find it. He wouldn't be able to stop me then.

Officer John was nearly there. I ran anyway. Maybe a few cuts between cars would buy me the time I needed to reach the bus. But Officer John was faster than he looked. I'd barely made the curve back toward the bus before his voice stalled me.

"Tank! Around back!" Then softer, "For the love of God, stop running, Mark."

I don't know why I stopped, but I did. This wasn't how any of it was supposed to go.

"On it!" The thunderous fall of Tank's steps carried along the fence, heavy grunts of "God-damn kids" broken into three words between heavier breaths.

By the time I faced him, Officer John was feet away, walking in a way that still seemed fast. I was glad to see the gun holstered again. "Where'd he go?"

"Huh?"

"Gordon! How did you all get in?"

"Bus," I said. "Middle back."

Officer John's hand hit my shoulder like an anvil. After an update on the radio, dispatch radioed back. Sirens blared in the distance. "What happened to his leg?"

"Knife. He attacked Reggie. He lost."

To my surprise, he chuckled, head side to side as if it came as no surprise. "Not an easy life, living in the home she does. Girl can defend herself, no doubt. Gordon won't get far. We'll find him, I promise, Mark. But I can't babysit you. Go home. Your mother's worried."

The thought of Mama brought a sharp pain. It was easier when I didn't have to think about what I'd done to her. "You're not taking me in?"

"Taking you in? For what?"

I hitched the pack. Showed off the bit of box sticking out because I couldn't say the words.

"God … no. Mark. I mean, that's an entirely different … No. Look, Gordon's into some bad things. Real bad. Go home. You and your mother have been through enough already. Doesn't need to be worse. All right?"

I took a moment. Not so much to give it thought, but because Officer John's look required it. "Yessir."

"I mean it." He cupped the back of my head like he was holding it in place, leveled down to meet me eye to eye. "I'm trusting you. Don't go there. Just take the ashes home and leave it be. Mitch is gone. The witch can't change that."

My expression gave me away. He nodded.

"Yeah, I know. Guessing Mitch told you. He asked me about her one night at your house. He said he'd heard the stories and wanted to know more. Didn't see any harm in it, so I told him what I tell anyone who asks. And I'll say the same to you now. It isn't worth chasing, Mark. What she does up there, it's a sin. She brings evil into the world. Bringing the dead back to life? You can't play God. Gone is gone. Let it be and move on. You aren't the only one who's lost someone. And you sure aren't the first to seek the witch. It won't end well. Trust me."

"But Zippy isn't—" Before I could finish, he ran off, scoping between cars as he made his way around the bend. Toward the bus.

He was wrong. Gone wasn't gone.

Zippy wasn't evil.

In no hurry, I headed toward the unguarded entrance, hitching my pack higher. It was heavier than before.

10

Mitch had been gone all night.

I flipped my pillow, for all the good it did. Both sides were gross with my tears and snot. I spent all day and night shut up in the room, pretending to be sick or asleep when Mama came in to check on me. Mitch said not to tell her about Zippy. That was Gordon's cross to bear. He said he'd take care of Zippy but left it at that, no matter my questions. Then he told Mama he was going camping at the Mall with some of his friends. Mama always let him go camping without any supervision. Of course, he was always good about being back on time the next morning, and always followed her rules, so I suppose he earned that trust. Mama wouldn't let me camp out unless Mitch was with me. Said I was too young. She always said that about everything. It felt like she didn't even notice I wasn't a kid anymore.

As he left, Mitch gave me a wave from the yard. I shut the curtains the moment he made his way down Moody, then crawled into bed. I didn't sleep much. Between my head blaring the repeated sound of the ball hitting Zippy and the memory of blood coating his beautiful white coat red, it was near impossible to even close my eyes.

It was early still when he came home, the house silent. Mama wouldn't wake for another hour or so. Soft steps bit against the wooden stairs, easing toward the front door. The screen creaked, door opened and shut gently. When the bedroom door parted free of the frame in a wobble, I wiped my face with the blanket and rolled over. Mitch snuck through the slim opening as if it might set off a bomb if opened any further, then closed the door behind him with a bare foot. All the while he kept his hands behind his back, the edge of the shoebox he'd used for Zippy peeking around one side.

Mitch looked exhausted. His face was lined with cuts. A few tears lined the sleeve of his white t-shirt, a bit of blood near the one highest on his shoulder. The pants of his jeans were filthy from the knee down, bare feet dirty and lined in dried mud at the ankle. He was always good about leaving his dirty socks and sneakers on the porch. Better than me.

"Sit up and don't say nothing," he said, more breath than voice. "Not a word, not a sound, you get me?"

I shot up without question, even though a good many lined up in a hurry. All of them to do with the scratching noises coming from the wobbly shoebox.

He made it to my bed in a few quick steps, box placed gently on the edge, hand pressed against the lid. Quarter-sized holes rounded the entire box, uneven, poked into place by a stick. Something inside gave the box a kick, a flash of fluffy white fur slipping into, then out of, sight through the holes. Mitch had to grab the box by the sides to keep it from falling to the floor. "Not a word," he repeated, gaze locked onto me like I might fall off the bed as well.

I could only nod and pull the blanket to my mouth. My throat tightened too much to attempt to speak, but it was better safe than sorry. The box rocked again, and more white fluff threaded into the holes. My heart raced. I couldn't help myself.

"Is that—"

His eyebrows raised and I pressed the blanket tighter against my mouth.

Gently, Mitch lifted the lid enough to slide his hand within. The thing in the box stopped moving, as if calmed by his touch. After a bit of wrangling, he pushed the top aside. I almost choked trying to hold back a shout. Mitch's fingers vanished into the unblemished white fur of the rabbit as he lifted it, its red eyes wide, back feet kicking for leverage but finding only air.

I didn't want to ask. I didn't want to be wrong. I didn't want to be a fool either, but it was getting harder by the second. "Zippy?" I could only whisper the name. It couldn't be.

He set the rabbit at my feet and I wrapped my hands around him before he could use the bed to kick off into a run. Mitch gave a short nod, the slightest crack of a smile rising at the corner of his mouth.

That was enough for me. Tears fell, in full force. My hands shook as I stroked Zippy's cotton-soft fur, from the tip of his wriggling nose to his fluffy tail. He looked good as new. As if no wrong had ever come to him. Mitch joined in, giving Zippy's head a sturdy scratch.

"How? He was ... I saw him, Mitch. He wasn't breathing. It's not possible."

For a few seconds that felt longer than a minute, Mitch played with Zippy's ears. He pulled them together then let them drop. "You ever hear of the witch on Spook Hill?"

"Witch?" I hugged Zippy so completely, I barely registered my own voice through all the fur. I could have hugged him for the rest of my life. But the word trickled into my brain and knocked around until I gave it my full attention. Until I followed what it meant. "There's a witch on Spook Hill? A real one? She brought him back?"

He winced, stood up, and walked to the window. The blinds rattled as he pulled the cord, but they rose in a lumpy mass of bent metal and held high. Light flooded the room from the rising sun peaking over the treetops. "I couldn't leave him like that. For him. For you. It wasn't right. Even God makes mistakes."

Zippy kicked again. This time I let him go. He bounded around the bed a few short hops, then stopped in the center and settled, red eyes on me, ears slicked back. He sure looked like Zippy, but he didn't spook as easy. He seemed content to hang out on the bed just fine.

"I never got this close to him at the ballfield. He always ran. You sure it's him?"

"I was there, wasn't I? Think I'm trying to fool you or something?" With a huff, Mitch collected Zippy and placed him carefully back in the box. Zippy seemed fine with it. Didn't even fuss when the lid dropped over him. "Not easy magic to bring a soul back, you know. For her, or for the one returning. Especially as time passes. She said four days was the most she'd do. Soul's still trying to come to grips with what's what. Hangs about. But by the fifth day, the soul's fine and ready to move on. Won't come back no matter what magic you use. Zippy was just gone the full day. Soul stays close to the body the first day. She said it'd only take a few days and he'd be back to normal."

Whatever tears I'd been fighting were gone. My cheeks tight, full of warmth. I realized the smile likely had everything to do with it. I couldn't remember feeling so happy. I embraced my brother in a leap, squeezed him with everything I could muster. "Thank you."

"You're welcome, Squirt. Just ... you gotta keep it between us, okay? Not your friends, not even Mama."

"I promise."

"She said nobody but you."

"I heard you. Nobody. I swear."

With a pat on my back, he pulled away. "Rad. Get dressed. Wear your old shoes. We're taking

Zippy to the Mall. He'll be safe there. Need to swing by the hardware store for some chicken wire. I'll leave a note for Mama, then grab a hammer and nails. Gotta build Zippy a cage and that back wall keeps coming loose at the corner. Told Dunk his father was short-cutting it. Don't want the whole place falling on us."

Without a word and faster than any time I could remember, I got dressed. Change went flying out of a pocket of my jeans as I snatched them off my dresser, a few coins rattling down the floor vent. Mitch drew to a full stop at the door, shoulders turned in. We waited, listened. The house stayed silent. Light glinting off a quarter on the floor sparked my thoughts in a new direction.

"Did it cost something?"

"What?" Mitch paused halfway out the open door. Didn't turn.

"The witch. Did she charge anything for it? I want to pay you back."

Mitch heaved a deep sigh, a look thrown over his shoulder. "Magic always has a cost. But it's mine to pay. Put your shoes on, all right? We'll talk about it on the way."

11

From the Junkyard, the only path to the Mall wasn't an easy one. We planned it that way. Best way to give up a secret hideout would be to leave it out in the open and call it what it was.

But after all the rain, the trip through the woods was brutal. Heat of day had already begun to creep in, wet turf spiking the humidity like a rising tide. The mucky ground sucked at my shoes with each step, the swampy smell overtaking everything else. Several more trees had fallen along and into the path, sheared limbs grabbing at the straps of my pack every time I ducked under or tried to crawl over. Thick gray clouds filled the sky, threatened more rain despite what the weatherman on channel five had said. Occasional bursts of wind rocked the tall pines, cones dropping as if trying to bomb me to oblivion.

All of which paled in comparison with the mosquitoes. Nothing but nature's vampires, made worse by a rainy month. By the time I reached the Mall I swore I'd been drained dry, arms and legs marked by a thousand bites I couldn't quit scratching.

The spot of woods we'd built the Mall in opened slightly, almost in a circle a good twenty yards wide. Grass rose high and thick, the soil not nearly as soppy. Mitch had used an axe to take down the one pine that sat near the center of the opening, leaving a stump we sanded down so that it was comfortable for two to sit on. We'd built a firepit near it, surrounded by rocks we scavenged from Edgewater Creek the time we'd ruined Mo's watch, for when the heat or rain wasn't making it impossible to enjoy. Three packs lined the stump, like a puffy rainbow of pillows. An open first aid kit lay by Reggie's. Dunk's was beside it, on its side, an open box of strawberry Pop Tarts poking out of the top. My stomach rumbled just seeing it.

The sight of the Mall, nestled between two towering pines, always gave me a spark of joy. It had held up well in the year since we finished the build. Mitch had taken some pointers from Dunk's dad, and a little help raising the walls, but all in all we built it ourselves. Getting the materials through the woods took a month's worth of weekends. Once summer break hit, the build went much faster.

Twin Pines Mall blared in painted red across a two-by-four header above the door, slightly faded, in need of some touch up. Dunk had come up with the name, citing the trees as well as the mall from *Back to the Future* as inspiration. Seemed perfect, though he spent the rest of the summer calling us all McFly and shouting, "Great, Scott!" and, "This is heavy," every chance he got.

The boxy design of the Mall came from the blueprints of a shed. We cut windows into the plywood walls on the front and back that propped open with one-by-ones four feet long. Rain sounded like a symphony in the hollow of the slightly steepled tin roof above the plywood ceiling, and the vent pipe running straight up the center groaned when heated from the fire pit inside. It was the only mall I'd ever been to. The only one I needed. Wasn't perfect by any stretch—the upkeep was constant—but walking into the clearing to see the door wide, my friends waiting, was all the reason to keep it going.

Reggie met me halfway, Dunk and Mo hovering behind, halfway through the sticky breakfast treats. A taped bandage ran the base of her throat, a thin red line a couple inches long staining through the fabric. Before my question could find a voice, she stopped it with an outstretched hand.

"It's fine. I've had papercuts worse. Just won't stop bleeding. What took you so long?" She pressed into the bandage, a little blood marking her palm. Without much thought, she stained the leg of her overalls with a quick wipe.

I walked past, eyeing Dunk and Mo as they chowed down. I wanted a Pop Tart like nobody's business. But it could wait. "Officer John."

"He caught you?" she asked, in step with me. "We saw you run, then we headed out the front. Thought you got out ahead of him."

"He wasn't after me. They were there for Gordon. He's into something bad."

Mo clapped his hands, a sharp sound that startled me to a stop short of the doorway. "Of course! Drugs. Don't you remember? That Senior? Barnaby ... Barney ... Barry ... I don't remember. Some name that makes you think of a tacky stained-cloth-wearing ogre that eats fair maidens. Or not so fair as things go around here. Oh, the stories my sister weaves. Anyway, he got busted last fall at school. LSD or coke or some other pedestrian nonsense."

"Cocaine," I said, the word drifting off like a puff of memory. "He never gave up his source though. He's still in jail. Officer John said something to Mama last night about Gordon dealing at school. I guess that's what he meant."

"I'll bet that's not all he talked to your mom about. *Brown chicken, brown cow!*" Dunk's odd rendition of music he claimed came from adult films ended in a wink, then he all but tripped over the packs trying to dance it off. His balance lost, he sandwiched what remained of his snack against Mo's shoulder in a strawberry-jam pastry-crumbled mess.

"Hey! Be careful, you barbarian! This tour shirt is sacred. The Goddess Madonna deserves more respect than smeared gelatin goo. Great. You jammed me. I don't carry Tide on my person, you know?"

Dunk wiped at it, doing nothing but spread the streak further. Mo slapped his hand away. "Eh, I'll bet she likes that kind of thing. See the way she dresses? 'Open Your Heart' didn't touch my heart, if you know what I'm saying."

"Gross." Reggie slugged him again in the shoulder, something that seemed to be part of every conversation they had these days. Sometimes it seemed he carried all the weight just to protect his shoulder from her punches.

Despite a throaty chuckle, Dunk rubbed the spot. "Sorry I missed the nut crunch you did on Gordo, by the way. Remind me never to face your direction when you're angry."

The memory of him toppling over made it impossible to keep the smile off my face. "Between that and the ninja move to bury the knife in his leg, I wouldn't expect him to take you on anytime soon."

She shrugged it off, fighting a losing battle against a wide grin. "Dad's army training, mostly. He's always on about the danger I'll be in, being a girl and all. I have to learn to protect myself. He always says, 'Kick 'em hard enough their future children feel it.' Guessing his poor sad sack of a grandson felt that one."

It took a few seconds, plus Reggie's grin, to set us to laughing. It felt nice to laugh. Then as fast it slipped away. Just like time. There wasn't enough of that left as it was. We had to get moving. According to the fluttering number on Mo's watch, it was almost 10:30. We were way behind.

The interior of the Mall was sparse, the air still and heavy. The blueprints we drew were tacked to one of the plywood walls, posters of Dale Murphy, Indiana Jones, Mötley Crüe, Whitesnake, Madonna, and the Bangles covering most of the others.

Aside from the space on the back-right wall, just above the window, it had held well. Mitch tried to nail the wall back in place several times, but it just wouldn't hold. He said the wall had warped from humidity too much to stick. Light cut through the thin gap and the wall wobbled every time we closed the door.

The patio carpeting—something I could swear was from Pirate's Cove, the old putt-putt course that closed—covered the ground, though we'd tracked in a good bit of sand. There was a firepit in the center, which Mitch insisted on no matter the dangers. It sank into the ground, two feet wide, rocks piled high, ash from the fire I burned two nights before marked by divots from the cup I used to collect some. The sight of it churned the thoughts again, tightened my stomach. The ashes in the baggie. The box in Mama's room. The swap. By now she knew. She'd be sick about it. Then furious. The moment she saw Mitch come home, though, she'd calm down. Maybe she'd even go easy on me.

Even if she didn't, it'd be worth it.

Zippy thumped a greeting from his chicken-wire pen along the side wall to the left, hay sprayed about with each kick. He did it every time I showed up. Pressed his nose into the wire until I reached over to stroke his white fur and give him a little scratch.

Mo closed the door before we had the shutters open, and the place dropped dark except for the sliver of light through the top of the wobbly wall.

Reggie moved quick to raise the shutter nearest the door, square cutout of plywood propped on the one-by-one, offering enough light for Dunk to open the other on the back wall. A breeze cut through the stuffy warmth, brought some fresh air to the stink of Zippy's waste.

Zippy hopped excitedly back and forth, then threw down another series of thumps. Like he was happy to see me. Happy to be alive. Thankful for what Mitch did. In all likelihood, though, he was just hungry. I poured some pellets from a bag beside the pen into his bowl, and he chowed down as if he'd gone psycho for food. Half his water in the dispenser was gone. I could stop by with Mitch on the way home to fill it.

I crouched to the pen, reached over the chicken wire to rub between Zippy's ears as he devoured his food. "You aren't evil, are you? Officer John doesn't know what he's talking about." Zippy stopped eating long enough to pierce me with his red eyes. To agree with me. Then he went back to eating.

"It doesn't creep you out?"

Took me a second to realize Dunk was talking to me. All three were looking my way, though not directly at me. "What?"

"That zombie rabbit."

"He's not a zombie, Dunk."

"You said he was dead, Murph. Now he's not. That's zombie territory to me."

The expected thud of Reggie's fist hitting Dunk's shoulder didn't come. Neither did Mo's shrill wit. Standing quiet beside him, they looked a bit scared.

"Zippy is not a zombie! He's alive. Like, normal alive! He's the same rabbit you've all petted and helped me feed and water for the past three months!"

Dunk snorted, almost choked on a laugh. "Yeah, but that was before we knew he was the Jesus of rabbits."

"The Jesus of … What?"

"Not the preachy bit. The raised from the dead part."

"He isn't dead! Well, I mean he was, but the witch brought him back."

"Right," nodded Dunk. "Was dead. Isn't now. Zombie Rabbit Jesus."

Mo clucked his tongue to his cheek. "Right. What he said. Minus the heresy. If it's true."

Reggie offered a shrug to my plea for back up. "They have a fair point. It's a bit out there."

Heat rose, burned my cheeks, sweat trickling past my ear. "Of course it's true! You think I'm lying to you? You think"—I tipped my pack over with the toe of my shoe, the corner of the box peeking out a bit more— "I'm doing all this for a laugh?"

"Nobody said you were lying," said Reggie, fingers all twisted through the straps of her overalls. For a moment she hung on a word, seemed to reconsider, then sighed. "It's just, well, you weren't there with Mitch, were you? It all seems a bit hard to believe, really."

Zippy kicked at the ground and I wanted to kick right along with him. The urge to grab my pack and storm out nearly took hold, but I pushed it away. "So, then you all think Mitch lied about it?" I took their silence as an answer. Gave me both a spike of anger and a knot of sadness. "I promise you, *that* is Zippy. Took him a week to get his strength back, but everything about him is the exact same as it was before. It's real. She *can* resurrect the dead. Mitch told me there were stories of her bringing back someone from only a fingernail. If I thought for a moment Mitch lied, I wouldn't be here. I'd be—"

—*at home accepting that Mitch was gone? That he was dead?*

I clamped my ears, hands pressed hard enough to squeeze loose the pressure in my head. To push the *d-word* away. Felt like a levee was about to break. Like soupy thought-water rising within, ready to spill over the top and pour from my eyes. I knelt back to Zippy to stroke his fur, if for no other reason than to keep my friends from seeing my fight against eyes that burned hot, threatening. "I need you to believe me. To believe Mitch. I have to do something. I'm the only one who can. Mitch would do the same for me. But I ... I don't want to go there alone. I don't want to face *her* by myself."

It seemed like the silence lasted an hour.

"Nah," Dunk said, a kick at the fake turf. "Nah. Of course Mitch wouldn't lie to you. Not about something like this. Would he?"

"Of course not," Reggie said in a rush, the edge of a smile barely showing itself. Hardly convincing.

I chanced a look at Mo. Dunk and Reggie both went wide-eyed at him. After one of his famous eye rolls—where it seemed like they stuck halfway, eyelids fluttering like mad—he took off his glasses long enough to rub his eyes. "Of course not. It's just"—glasses back on, eyebrows raised, he scanned the interior, arms wide—"as Lady Madonna would say ..."

"Here we go." Dunk crossed his arms, amused, waiting.

"Mo, not now." I knew the bit. Knew what song he was about to launch into. He sang it to us every chance he got. Often when things were at their suckiest. But I wasn't in the mood and we needed to get rolling.

Mo cleared his throat, encouraged by my protest. "Life—"

"I keep saying," Dunk said, bringing Mo to a cold stop. "'Eternal Flame' is a thousand times better than 'Like a Prayer.' Do that one. I'll sing to that. Any time you want."

For a moment, Mo looked like he'd been shot. Hand to his chest, eyes wide, pained as he staggered toward the poster of Madonna. "'Like a Prayer' is the single greatest song ever written. Period. The End. Hallelujah, amen. How can you compare a mere mortal—lovely though Susanna Hoffs may be—to the angelic voice of Aphrodite? You can't. It's pure idiocy. This is why you don't have a girlfriend."

103

"Yeah? Well, then I'm a blissful lonely idiot in love with Susanna Hoffs. I can live with that." Dunk joined me at the pen, laughing until he caught my eye. He hesitated, shrugged, then petted Zippy. Reggie crowded beside him, offered me another smile that didn't last. "So, what's the plan, Murph? Or would you like to whistle a few bars of 'Walk Like an Egyptian' with me first?"

Mo's huff was as much an apology to the poster of Madonna as anything. He landed a cheek to the print, hand to her hair. "They don't understand. You're a treasure."

The map was a bit more crinkled than before, folded several times over to fit in my back pocket. I pressed it hard to unfold it on the floor, marking the trail with a finger. "There. It's a bit of a walk still, but once we find that trail, we follow it straight to 100. Cross the bridge over Edgewater Creek to Spook Hill, up some road, and we're there. I'm guessing this number is an address."

Reggie's chin touched my shoulder as she studied Mitch's drawing. I tried not to react, but she never usually got so close. Weird though it was, a good part of me hoped she'd stay that way a while. The rest of me just shouted about not thinking of my friend that way, even if I'd seen her in a dress. As if she'd heard my thoughts, she drew back a bit. "Then what?"

"Then we see the witch, I guess. And I give her this." The card withdrew easily from underneath my shirt, twirling at the end of the shoelace.

"The baseball card from Gordon's car?" asked Dunk.

As if it helped explain it better, I moved it closer. "Not just any card."

Reggie caught it between her fingers. Her nails were longer than I remembered. They were still red from where she painted them for the memorial. "That's the one you lost to him, right? The bogus bet."

From his toes, Mo hovered over the other side of the map, passing a look at the card. "Bogus bet?"

"Gordon and Mitch were on different baseball teams, in the championship. Gordon was pitching," Reggie said before I could. When our gazes met, she smiled and gave a nod for me to finish the story.

"Mitch's team was down a run in the last inning. He was due up third. Gordon was running his mouth before he went out to the mound, like always. Said he'd strike out the side, Mitch included. So, I told him that Mitch would get a hit off him. Gordon bet me he wouldn't. He wanted the card if he was right. Knew it was my favorite. But I didn't see a way I could lose. Mitch always got hits off Gordon. Every single at bat. Homers, a lot of the time. He'd seen all his pitches for years. Knew what was coming as if he'd called it himself. Had him timed perfectly."

Mo inched closer. "So, he didn't get a, um, thing—"

"A hit," said Reggie.

"Yeah, that."

I tucked the card away again, embarrassed to say it in front of Dale Murphy's smiling face. "No. First two guys struck out. Mitch came up. Could have tied it with a homer, but Gordon walked him on four pitches. All but threw them straight to the backstop just to avoid giving him a pitch to hit. Then he struck the last batter out to end the game."

Mo stared a moment, then shrugged. "And that's bad?"

"He pitched around him?" Dunk whistled. "Lame-o way to win a bet. He didn't get a hit. But he didn't get him out either."

Mo continued to stare, blinking as if in code. "Explain it to me like I have no idea about anything baseball. Because I don't."

"He cheated," added Reggie, with a shake of the head that would have shamed the devil. "Add that to his list of charms."

"Ah," said Mo, with far less enthusiasm than showed on his face. "So, if he cheated, why give him the card?"

I shrugged. "Mitch insisted I own up. He was mad as all get out at Gordon for cheating me, and for pitching around him, but he wouldn't let me refuse. Took me straight home to get it."

"So, why are you giving the witch that card?" Mo asked.

I busied myself doing a whole lot of nothing with the zipper on the pack. I hadn't exactly covered this part of the story yet. They weren't going to like it one bit, but it was the way it had to be. No way I'd try to hide it.

"There's a cost to bringing someone back. The witch says this kind of magic can mess up the balance between life and death. So, she has to have something that means a lot to someone. Something they keep real close. Something like this card. To bring Zippy back, Mitch said he took a chew toy from the Herberts' dog, Bonzo. Animal for an animal, he said. It was sick anyway. When he died a few days later, nobody thought anything of it. But the witch didn't know that. The toy was Bonzo's favorite. Always had it nearby. He bit a kid once who tried to take it. Not sure how Mitch got it from him, but he did. So, that's why I needed the card."

Reggie stood fast enough to startle Zippy into a hay-kicking sprint around his pen. "You're passing the cost off to Gordon?"

"It's his to pay," I said simply, unable to face them.

Mo's hand found his chest again. He spoke in a whisper, like doing much else would allow God to hear. "You mean he would die? Is that what you're saying? You're going to have her kill him?"

I looped the pack over my shoulder and folded up the map. Looking up to meet Mo's wide dark eyes was near impossible, but I did it quick. Then, as fast, I found some interest in mud on my shoes. "It should have been him to begin with. He was the one who ran the stop sign."

The three of them stood frozen, mouths open like they were in a contest to see who could be the most horrified. But I couldn't bend on this one, no matter how awful it sounded. It was Gordon or Mitch. Only one choice as I saw it.

"He threw a baseball at Zippy and killed him! He's the reason Mitch is—" Something bit at my insides and I swallowed it back, the word dying with it. "He would have killed you too, Reg! You know it! You all saw how crazy he went when he saw I had the card!"

The butt of Gordon's gun pressed into my back. Like that heartbeat in the floorboard in the Poe story we read in English, giving away that it wasn't the card Gordon was upset over. I tried to shift the pack to silence it, but the gun moved with it, slipping the strap from my shoulder. The pack caught in the crook of my elbow, the map knocked free. It dropped to the floor, the pack swaying above like the pendulum of a clock.

Dunk teetered his head side to side. "Not going to argue how crazy he is, Murph. Cops aren't after him for the fun of it. But … you sure you want to do this?"

"You're playing God." Mo's chin rose. Just like his mama when she talked Jesus at us.

"Playing God? He's the one who played God! He's selling drugs, right? So, what if he was high when he was driving? What if that's why he ran the stop? Mitch didn't deserve what happened!"

When they held quiet, I shouldered the pack. I waited, hoping they'd go along with it. But they didn't say a word and the worry crept in. "I have to do this. I have to. I'm really sorry I didn't tell y'all about the card, or why I needed it. I am, I swear. Please come with me. Please. Gordon has to pay."

A laugh penetrated their silence. From outside the Mall. Made me sick. Made my entire body tense. I didn't need to peek out the window to know who it was.

12

ordon gave a smug smile. Pushed Dunk's pack over and smashed the open box of foil-covered Pop Tarts on the ground with the tip of the Easton.

"You keep saying that, runt nuts. I gotta pay. But I don't see you doing anything about it."

His pant leg was soaked red, stain running like a river into his sock, but he'd taken his shirt off and tied it tight against the wound. When he moved, he hobbled a bit and winced, barrel of the bat planted into the earth to give him some balance. His chest heaved with each breath, with each shot of pain, lean muscle stretching skin that glistened with sweat. Long cuts and wide scabs covered a good bit of his shoulder and side. The accident did more damage to him than I thought.

"Bunch of goobs. You're all loud enough for a deaf person to follow. Now, look. It's simple. You've got something of mine. I want it back. Do it and we're done."

For all the good it did, I wished I'd left the gun where it was. If I had, he wouldn't have attacked Reggie, he wouldn't have the Easton, and he wouldn't have followed me. I couldn't let him stop us, but there was no chance we'd get out of the Mall and on the run before he made a move. Even hobbled, even with his shoulder messed up, he'd catch us. Or at least one of us, which was enough for me. Without much thought, I fastened the latch on the door. Wouldn't do much more than keep it in place for a short bit. Gordon would bust through it with little effort.

"Oh, man, Murph. I knew you were dumb, but this is ridiculous. Now I have to take it out of your hide."

He was right. It *was* stupid, but I had no choice.

"What are we going to do?" Mo's voice pitched high enough to cut into my ears.

"I don't ... I don't know." Other than small rocks around the pit, we didn't have anything in the Mall to fight with. Never thought we'd have to. Once he got inside, he'd be on us before the rocks did much good.

Gordon's laugh fell soft, but somehow louder than my heartbeat. "Homey little place you have here. Mitch mentioned it plenty but wouldn't tell me where it was. Is this where I get to be the Big Bad Wolf? Little piggies, little piggies, and shit?"

He thumped a solid hit to the wall with the bat, a testing blow that still gave the entire structure a shimmy. Mo's squeal hit a new high, but it wasn't much worse than the rest of us. We crowded away from the door, toward the back as he swung full-on. The tin roof rattled.

"Last chance, Murph. Open the door or I may bring this whole piece of crap down on top of you."

The Mall wobbled with another strike, this time splitting a crack into the door. The latch rattled but didn't give. The shake of the walls knocked the one-by-one free of the back window, the clap of which scared the piss out of us. It went dark on that side, except for the sliver of light near the ceiling.

"Getting closer, Murph. Doesn't look solid enough to take much more."

"The window," said Reggie, a hard tug to my sleeve. "We can go out the back and take off when he comes in. Might give us enough time."

"Good idea!" Mo wasted no time discussing it. Despite the flap of plywood bouncing against his back, he hurled himself into the opening, struggling to swing a leg through. "I'll get out and hold it open!"

The door buckled with another hit and the crack in the plywood door widened. The screws holding the latch to the wall pulled, almost popped loose.

Mo cleared the window, dropped free in a painful thud, the shutter bouncing shut behind him. After a second or two he reappeared, shutter held as high as he could get it. "Let's go!"

"Except ..." I paused, gave Dunk an apologetic look. I didn't want to say it then, even more than I didn't want to say it at the bus. "You need to go before we do. We can ... push."

"Nah." He waved it off. "Y'all go without me. Been working on my charge. I can buy you some time. Dad says I'll make a great lineman. Probably take out a few quarterbacks someday. All about lowering the shoulder and using my weight." He patted his stomach, which gave a sharp *crack*. "I got plenty of that."

"Duncan, we're not leaving you!" I'd never seen Reggie scared before. Strangely, the way the blush hit her olive skin made her look furious.

There wasn't time to debate. Gordon's next hit—likely a kick, based on the impact—sent the entire Mall into a lean a half a foot back. More light poured through the top of the back wall

"Come on!" yelled Mo.

Reggie turned to the window, but I grabbed her arm. Nodded to the light. "No, wait! The wall. Where it's pulled away. We just have to wait until he's inside."

The gap shifted wider with another hit from Gordon, running from the corner to near halfway along the wall. Reggie looked back at me, clearly not getting it. But Dunk smiled wide. "Like a quarterback?"

"Totally. Hold my pack!" I gently handed Mo my pack, sure to give him only the straps, then rushed to grab Zippy. He protested, kicked a few times as I lifted, but settled the moment I brought him to my chest.

Dunk set his feet, faced the back wall, shoulder down. "Just remember that my love for food saved us all. I'll take the center. You two take the ends. Wait for my signal. Keep low, lead with your shoulder. Or with the back of your shoulder, Murph, unless you're using the zombie rabbit as a battering ram."

Reggie finally got a grip on what we were saying. "No, no, no, no. This is a *bad* idea."

"Maybe," I said, fumbling a bit on my grip of Zippy. "Only one way to find out. Clear back, Mo. Way back." Mo cut away fast, clearly in Camp Reggie with the plan. Before Gordon could land another kick, I sped to the door and freed the latch. "Hold up, okay? I'll give it to you. Just don't kick the place down."

After a silent moment, the door opened, barrel of the Easton leading it wide. Gordon's arrogant smile spread across his face. "No games. Hand it … What the hell is with you and rabbits anyway? How about you put it down and let me see if I can crack its skull with this bat? That'd be good fun for everyone."

I pressed the anger back. He wasn't getting another shot at Zippy. "The rabbit stays with me." We gathered at the front of the firepit, steps away from Gordon, leaving a bit of distance to the wall. I swallowed hard. If it didn't work, it would hurt like the dickens. Of course, if it didn't work, Gordon's response was going to hurt worse, so we had little to lose in trying.

As soon as he cleared the doorway, I let a deep breath fly free.

A step.

Another step.

"Now!"

Dunk's shout rose like the wail of a tornado siren. There wasn't enough room to get any real speed, but the three of us hit the wall as hard as we could, driving into the plywood. Truth be told, Dunk did the work. He hit the wall screaming, hands extending as his shoulder collected the plywood to add to his leverage. When I hit the wall, I felt like a moth bouncing off a light. I managed to protect Zippy during the impact, but the moment the nails pulled free at the top and the plywood gave way, he kicked hard. His claws dug into my shirt and tore at my skin. I somehow held on despite the pain, back to the wall as it fell. Most of the base ripped free of the framing along the ground, plywood and two-by-fours splintered at the nails like cracked celery.

The entire Mall bucked, the pull of the wall lurching it our way. For a second it looked like the entire plan was going to backfire, the whole structure toppling down on us as we lay on top of the fallen wall, but the twin pines squeezed the side walls and brought it to a stop, into a full lean. It wobbled a bit but held.

Better, but not at all helpful.

"Jesus Christ!" Gordon laughed, somewhere between hysterics and humor. "You little bastards are insane!" He tapped the ceiling with the bat, laugh coming a bit easier, then landed a sharp gaze on me. "Ain't gonna matter much, though. Except for the part where I have to hurt you for it."

With a devilish grin, Gordon charged, bat raised.

All I could think was that it couldn't happen to Zippy again. I let go. With another painful kick to my chest, he scampered across the wall to freedom. I watched him hop away, toward the woods, knowing I'd never see him again.

But at least he'd be alive.

"No!"

Reggie's scream pulled me back. She jumped to her feet, stepping between me and Gordon, arms over her head to shield against any blow of the bat. If her sacrifice registered with Gordon at all, it didn't show. He didn't alter his path a bit, bat cocked all the way around, ready to crush whatever it hit, eyes wild and as wide as could be.

Then he stopped cold, cheeks paled in a rush. The Easton dropped from his grip, issued a solid *clunk* on the indoor carpet behind him. When he screamed it sounded like all the worst curse words combined into one. It wasn't until his hands dropped, cupping either side of his knee that I realized what had happened.

The razor-sharp point of a ten-penny nail poked just out from the top of the muddy white of his Adidas. A wave of red spread along the shoe-laces, stained the toes of the shoe. His scream faded into a choppy breath as he rocked to maintain balance on a gimpy leg that had already worn a blade to the thigh.

Pulling on his leg carefully like it might break, Gordon tried to lift his foot. When it wouldn't budge, he hobbled a bit, shifting the nail enough to draw another scream. The nail was wedged too tight into the sole of his shoe, and a second attempt only brought the two-by-four framing up with it. Breath coming in deep gasps, he tried to regroup, but the pain seemed to be taking him whole and his good leg buckled. He stumbled backward, eyes rolling up. When he fell, it looked like the framing along the ground might go with him, the nail still buried through his foot. Then it snapped back, and his shoe slipped free. The framing clapped the ground in a rattle.

Gordon managed to stagger a few steps, wailing each time his wounded foot landed. Somewhere on the verge of passing out, he made one more move our way. But the first step landed square on the barrel of the Easton. His ankle twisted as the bat rolled sharp to the side. The second his bloody foot planted to brace him, he recoiled, and the battle for balance was over. He fell backward, shoulders and head slamming into the front wall, the added weight tugging the Mall away from us.

This time the twin pines didn't hold.

The entire structure collapsed forward in a groaning lean, loud as a tree falling as it landed, Gordon pinned beneath.

From under the broken mass of plywood, tin roof, and splintered two-by-fours, Gordon's legs were visible. His blood-soaked shoe twitched. Part of the ceiling rose an inch or so with each breath. He was out cold but alive, which was all I needed to know.

He couldn't die yet.

But staring upon the wreckage of the Mall gave me one more reason to finish the job. The place that meant so much to us, so much to me and Mitch, was destroyed. Brought down because of Gordon. Because of everything he'd done so far. It was all his fault. If not for Gordon, everything would be fine. Everything would be normal.

Mitch would have come home.

"Holy hell," said Dunk, beside me on the fallen wall. "That was righteous."

"You okay?"

Took me a few seconds to realize Reggie was talking to me. When I finally turned away from the remains of the hideaway Mitch helped us build, her hand was there. Waiting for mine. I grabbed it. When she pulled me to my feet, I couldn't hold her stare. "He would have hit you. I ... You—"

"—did what any of us would have done. We're in this together." Her voice dropped and she dusted a whole lot of nothing off her overalls. "You need to get to Spook Hill. For Mitch. For you."

"Oh my God, oh my God, oh my God, oh my God." Mo draped himself across me and Reggie, my pack still looped over his elbow. I grabbed it before the gun could bounce against her back. "Can we please, please, leave now?"

The Easton lay along the back-wall framing, near the blood-soaked nail that had pierced his foot. "We definitely don't want to be here when he wakes up, so yeah. Let's grab our stuff and find the trail."

Reggie and Dunk eased around the fallen hideout, slow to their packs, eyes on Gordon.

Mo didn't move. His mouth hung open, glasses low on the tip of his nose. "Trail? You're still going to the witch? After all this? We have to go to the police, Mark! Jason Vorhees over there is going to wake up at some point and chase us down. I don't think he's going to want to talk about it."

"We'll be too far off at that point. He'll never find us."

"That's what those dopey-eyed goons say just before Jason guts them with a machete! He doesn't ever die either, in case you missed it."

"Gordon isn't Jason! This is real life, not a movie!"

"Exactly! It's real life! With real blood, and real pain, and an idiot who wants us to have plenty of both! And there isn't some mythical witch living on some poorly named hill who can bring back Mitch! He's dead, Mark!"

The wild look in his eyes faded almost as fast as it rose, but the *d-word* lingered in my head, poking, prodding, tormenting. Reggie and Dunk shuffled behind Mo with the packs, each staring into me as if waiting for me to start swinging.

I didn't have time to argue. Or to listen to nonsense.

"If you don't want to go, then fine. Go home!" I pushed past Mo with a shoulder, knocking him a few steps back. The tacky feel of the Easton's grip in my hand eased my anger a bit. I collected my friends in what I hoped was a calm stare.

But I knew I'd missed the target. I could see it in their reaction. Not sure they'd ever seen me that mad before. Didn't happen often as it was. Mitch always said a calm head ruled over chaos. But calm wasn't happening. Calm lay in a broken pile where a hideout used to stand. "You can all go home if you want. Mitch isn't ... He just isn't. I don't need you to believe me."

"Mark." Reggie tried to grab me by the shoulder as I walked past, but I dipped beneath and kept walking.

I couldn't tell who followed me. No one spoke. I didn't look back. I just heard the trailing crunch of leaves as I left the broken remains of our hideout behind and knew I wasn't alone.

13

We walked a while without a word. The narrow path was one Mitch and I had walked a number of times, though only a short section while looking for wood to burn. I'd never gone this far. It cut straight through the heart of broadleaf trees, worn down to the soil. In between the tromping of our steps, bird cries mixed with the chatter of squirrels. The grey blanket of clouds cut into the usual blast of June heat, but not enough. The humidity had us drenched from head to toe. The bloody patch on my stomach from Zippy's claws had darkened and spread into the sweaty white fabric of my shirt. The thought of Zippy running off bit into my brain. Every bit as sharp-clawed as his fuzzy feet. It was a strange and horrible thought, knowing I'd probably never see him again. Somehow felt worse than the day at the ballfield.

My throat tightened. I pushed it all away.

The path rose slightly, low hanging branches and prickly brush slowing passage to a one-by-one squeeze in spots, vines and exposed roots catching shoelaces in others. Reggie had to call for me to stop a handful of times. I stopped for her but wouldn't look back to see who was bent tying a shoe. Instead, I calmed the voices in my head by practicing my swing with the Easton, clipping the tips of a few branches.

Sweat stretched the neckline of my t-shirt. No matter how many times I pulled at the sleeves, it'd slip back down below my collar bones. Between that and the plastic sheath of the baseball card sticking to my chest, the frustration about drove me to a fussing fit. Finally, I gave up, pulled the card outside my shirt, and let the neckline droop.

Wasn't until Dunk spoke, words broken by his labored breath, that I knew for sure all three of my friends were back there.

"I've been thinking about it, Mo. Gordon isn't Jason at all. Jason has some magic mojo that gets him where he needs to be, sure, but he's just lucky, mostly. Dumb campers are always running right to him. Gordon's not lucky at all—I think we can all agree on that—and we sure aren't dumb. Nah, he's the Borg. Relentless, heartless, all kinds of firepower, all about us not resisting him."

"What's a Borg?" Mo fought a bit with the walk as well, winded less than Dunk, but winded all the same. Between the slow rise of the woods and the packs we carried, it was a wonder we could talk at all.

Sure seemed simpler when I was planning it.

"New species on *The Next Generation*. Militant robot-human dudes that turn other species into more militant robot-whatever dudes. They just want to conquer and destroy because they can, basically."

"Is that the show you forced me to watch that has the unfortunate woman in the hideous mauve jumper that does her figure no favors?"

"Who, Troi?"

Mo's shrug somehow had volume to it. Like a sigh meeting a cough, whispered on a sharp breeze. Or maybe I just knew him too well to need to see it.

"Not like it's her fault," said Reggie. "She's the ship's counselor, not an officer. She can't wear the uniform. Unfair, if you ask me."

"So, she has to be punished? Honestly, is there not a pants suit she could wear instead? The future is so uncivilized. If that's what we have to look forward to, I want no part of it."

"You want no part of space exploration and meeting new species?" asked Dunk.

"Not if we still have tacky figure-inflating jumpers, no. The current abuse of hair spray is enough, thank you."

In the silence that returned, a faint sound carried through the trees. Like static from a television.

"You saw that episode, right Murph? The one where Q sent the *Enterprise* across the galaxy just by snapping his fingers?"

For a moment, I considered not answering. But I wasn't mad at Dunk, and it was a pretty damn good episode. "Hell, yeah," I said, scouting the trail ahead. There was less of it than before, grass and weed closing in, leaving dirt less than a foot wide. Beyond, the way was blocked by a mammoth fallen oak. It was hard to tell, but it looked as though the path didn't clear up after. The forest just swallowed it, choking it off entirely. There had to be another way. If Mitch made it, then he had to have gone another direction. I headed off-path, working my way around the root side of the tree. "The Borg were a cool add," I said, barely registering it.

"They were totally excellent is what they were. I mean, this season was already bombdiggity—well, except for Pulaski. I miss Crusher, even though she reminds me too much of my mom. Anyway, could you imagine? One minute you're in a part of space you know, then blammo! You're somewhere you've never been, with no star chart to get home, or any idea where to even go from there. Plus, there's these crazy cyborgs hunting you down. Nutso."

A flare shot through my thoughts.

"Star chart?"

The words barely out, I stopped just past the base of the tree. Fast enough that Reggie ran into me. My heart skipped a few beats, in an unnatural hurry to race its way out of my chest. I patted my pockets, though I knew I'd find nothing there. "Damn."

Dunk whistled. "Righteous. Just ripped right out of the ground, didn't it? Check out the roots. Wide as my arm." As if we needed the proof, he stretched his arm along a root. His arm wasn't close. The root was twice as thick.

"Not that," I said, tapping the tree mindlessly with the knob of the bat. A busted branch extended several feet out from the trunk, a foot wide, enough to hold my weight and give me a boost. Atop the trunk, I could see further off. The path was there, but only for another twenty feet or so. Then it became a tangle of trees, ivy, and brush.

Reggie joined me. "Think it's past all that? Has to pick up again somewhere, right? What's the map say?"

I dug my free hand in every pocket, as much for show as to buy me a few seconds of thought. It wasn't there. I knew that much. "No idea. I dropped it, remember? Just before Gordon showed up?"

Mo gave a short gasp but fought back whatever rant tried to bubble up.

"You don't have the map?" asked Reggie.

I shook my head, which suddenly felt loose, bobbing on a swivel. I thought it might just pop free and fall off. "Got busy knocking the place down so we could get away, didn't we?"

Mo went shrill, level five in a hurry. "So, you don't know where we're going? We're in the middle of the woods with no idea where to go? Is that what you're saying, Murph?"

I shrugged, no desire to watch Mo work his way into another meltdown. The fact that it'd be justified was enough to spike the tone in my response. "Yeah, I know where we're going. Same place as before. Just not on a clear path, I guess. Mitch drew the map. Path was straight from the Mall, headed northwest. We follow that to 100."

"Then where's the path? Why did he draw a thing that wasn't there?" His hands were on his hip, brows raised above the frames of his glasses.

Reggie nudged me with an elbow. Bit at her lip like she always did when the nerves got the best of her. Didn't happen often, but when it did, I knew I had to step up. I took a breath, trying to find some sense of calm that didn't exist. "He didn't draw anything about it ending. Maybe he just meant that we continue northwest until the path shows again. He had a bunch of cuts and scrapes, so he must have worked his way through the undergrowth. Either that, or the path peeled off and we didn't notice."

"Well, we sure as hell can't go back," said Reggie, in a leap from the trunk.

"The Borg will assimilate us."

Mo glared at Dunk.

"I meant that Gordon—"

"I know what you mean, Dunk. I don't have to be a future-loving dorkis to figure out what running straight to the bad guy will mean. Jason, remember?"

Dunk gave a thumbs up, smile wide. "Right on, dude."

"So, what? We take our chances finding the path?" asked Reggie.

I took another deep breath, adjusted the pack to my other shoulder. It felt heavier. The spot where the strap had laid burned. If I didn't know better, I'd have sworn my friends were adding rocks to it as I walked.

The Easton gave a hollow *thunk* when I tapped the trunk. Wind rustled the treetops. When it died, the static took over. Faint. Distant. Constant. Almost like a waterfall.

"The overpass on 100!"

They stared at me.

"The sound? Can't you hear it? It's water."

Reggie cupped her ear. Mo followed her lead. Dunk looked around, then swatted at a bug.

"Edgewater?" asked Reggie.

"Yes! Edgewater Creek!" I worked my way down off the trunk with less skill or grace than I'd hoped. "We don't have to look for the path. Just head to the creek and follow it to 100. The overpass is there. We can work our way onto the road and cross."

14

It was easier said than done.

Pines, oaks, and hickory lay thick, brush and overgrowth filling the space between. Swings of the Easton cleared a good bit of thorny vines in our path, but more than once we had to peel back further south to get around rough patches. Were we moving in any other direction, I'd have worried about getting lost. Fortunately, the growing sounds of the creek eased any concern. One way or another, we'd get there.

After about an hour, Dunk started moaning and wailing about being hungry, flopping into every tree like he'd ooze into a puddle without its support. It wasn't anything new. We'd seen it countless times. Usually, he'd go it alone because the rest of us had eaten enough to satisfy our stomachs, but this time was different. Mo was dragging his feet, complaining to high heaven about how dirty his sneakers were getting, and Reggie had gotten a bit punchy.

So, between the hunger and our sore shoulders from her solid hits, we had no choice but to stop. I thought Dunk might just eat the box the Pop Tarts came in before we could open a pack. From his folks' pantry, he'd also grabbed a box of Little Debbie jelly rolls, a bag of Lay's, and packs of cheese and cracker sandwiches. I'm not sure how long he thought we were going to be gone, but leave it to Dunk to have filled his pack with an entire pantry.

Mo had Juicy Juice boxes in his pack. There were only six—all he was willing to swipe knowing his mom would light into him enough as it was—but it did for the moment. We'd just have to make do on the way back with nothing to drink.

For a time, there wasn't any conversation. No looks at one another. Mostly, just a lot of staring into the woods, following the flight of birds, or drawing doodles in the soil exposed between clumps of grass. I cradled my pack, following a jelly roll with some cheesy crackers, and plinked the aluminum bat with a fingernail to keep my mind at bay. It kept wandering into dark places I didn't want it to go.

Gordon's bashed up car. The stained seat. Mitch's empty bed the morning after. Mama crying her way through telling me what happened. Why he wasn't home.

I wanted to clock my head with the bat until it all stopped.

Mostly, I just wanted to get on with the trip.

When I finally pulled out of my thoughts, I found Reggie staring at me. She didn't look away. Just kept staring, like she was reading my thoughts. She did that a lot, but there was something different about it this time.

"Kinda crazy to think we'll be in high school in another year," she said.

Mo just gave a shrug, but Dunk jumped on it. "I'm not ready for it yet. I mean, yeah, I am, but let's rule the roost a bit next year before we get dropkicked back to the bottom, right? We're not the newbie sixth graders anymore. We're cool eighth graders."

I almost snorted. "Cool? There's nothing cool about us, Dunk. We're the dorks everyone picks on no matter what grade we're in."

"Speak for yourself, Murph. I'm large and in charge." As if he needed to drive the point home, he crammed two Pop Tarts into his mouth at once.

"Aw, that's just repulsive, Dunk," said Mo, hand out to block his view of Dunk's pastry-and-jam-covered face. "You keep that up and you'll definitely be large. Er."

If anything, Dunk celebrated it with a slap to his gut and a laugh that showed way too much of what he was working so hard to swallow.

"I hope we'll all still know each other," Reggie said, busying herself picking at some grass. "When we're in high school."

"Of course we will," I said, without giving a thought otherwise. Seemed a kinda dumb thing to say. Not that I'd ever say such a thing to Reggie.

"Hope so."

The good thing about knowing someone so long is that you learned to see more than they gave. I'd known Reggie for a few months more than six years. She wasn't one to hope for anything. She tended to just go get what she wanted and leave the hope to other people.

"Why wouldn't we be?"

"I don't know," she said, a half shrug guiding her. "Things happen. People grow apart. Sometimes family gets in the way."

"Family's what you make, not what you're born with," said Mo. The pointed tone he usually carried softened a bit. "Don't tell my mom I said that. She runs our family reunions like a church service."

We met eyes for a second, then looked away. "We're friends. Nothing's changing that. Not eighth grade, not high school, not anything." With all that I'd dealt with over the past few days, this was something I didn't want to give a second of fight to. "Why would family get in the way? Mama loves all of you. Says so all the time."

"Shoot," said Dunk, still working a mouthful of food, "my mom can't stop talking about you guys. Though she's set on making sure you and Mo get some food in you. Just, you know, in case you're over for dinner anytime soon."

Reggie found a stick and stabbed the ground with it. "Just ..." She shrugged. "I don't know. Some parents may not be as understanding. They might see me hanging out with three boys and think funny things. They might say I need to find some girlfriends before people start talking about my reputation."

"That's stupid," shot Dunk. "Who'd say that?"

But I knew who. And it brought me to my feet. Sent a wave of anger through me like a furnace. Reggie didn't talk much about her home life. I think I was the only one who had ever set foot inside her house. Her daddy hadn't been happy about it either.

"Well," I said, trying to measure my words the way Mitch would have, "you can tell your .... You can tell *him* that *we* know you. Better than anyone. We know how good and how strong you are, and if anyone says otherwise, they'll have us to deal with. Him included."

"Amen," said Mo, on his feet as well.

Dunk stumbled a bit trying to stand, but managed with Mo's help, his throaty "hell, yeah" carrying into the forest like gunshot.

Reggie flinched, her gaze combing across the three of us, and for a moment I thought she might tear up. But she never teared up. Not once in the time I'd known her. So, when she hopped to her feet, smiling a smile that showed no sign of embarrassment or shame, it didn't surprise me.

Only person I knew that carried themselves with more strength was Mitch. It was no wonder she was my friend.

"We should go, right?" she asked, already gathering her trash and stuffing it into a pouch of her pack.

15

By the time the creek showed between the trees, I realized why I could hear it so well. Three days of rain had swollen the trickling water—one we'd all waded in closer to town without getting more than calf deep more times than I could count—into a rapid flow. Normally about ten feet wide, the rains had spread the creek another ten, easy. The water rose well past its boundary, flowing above the bank on both sides, carrying away soil and debris like melting ice. We found some higher ground between two oaks, where the overflow spilled out less. Water ran gently into one of the trunks, enough to clear the topsoil and expose its roots.

"Must be a good four feet deep, you think?" asked Dunk.

"Definitely," said Reggie. "Look at the trees over there, in the center."

About fifty yards downstream, a narrow island of young oak saplings centered the creek, remaining trunks shivering against the force of the rapidly flowing water. It served as a collection point, accumulating trash and branches, water foaming as it churned. One of the trees had snapped beneath the water line, the thin trunk stretched across the water toward the opposite bank, swaying as if trying desperately to hold on. Not much further, a thick pine stretched entirely across the creek, keeled over from the opposite bank, its root structure splayed for all to see.

With all the water pouring over the bank, we'd have to backtrack a bit and force our way through the brush until we reached 100 or found another path. It wouldn't be an easy trip. The undergrowth was thick. Brambles added to an already difficult passage. We'd have to keep further from the creek than I'd expected. But it was the only choice left.

"Uh. Guys?"

His voice was shrill. Quivered ever so slightly. I didn't need to turn to know Mo had discovered something we wouldn't like. I fully expected to see Gordon approaching, bloody leg and all.

But it wasn't Gordon.

I'd rather it had been.

Mo stood well off, near a clear patch between a cluster of trees, bits of grass and vine pockmarking the ground. The soil looked as though it had been combed with a hoe. Spread all about. Little tufts of something half buried by soil moved in the breeze. At first, I thought it was fur, and images of Zippy meeting a horrible end nearly stopped my heart. But as I closed in, cautious steps pulling me even with Mo, I could see it wasn't fur at all.

It was feathers. Some torn, some whole, plucked free and scattered. A few had streaks of blood. It looked like a chicken had exploded. In the center of the scene, the soil went darker. Wetter. Paw prints two or three times the size of my hands headed off in line, even with the creek. Rainwater pooled in the prints. Fresh. Too fresh.

"Please tell me I'm not seeing this. It's a mirage from being outdoors too long, right? Because if it isn't, I'm going to lose my Pop Tart."

Dunk surveyed the sight, whistled, then patted Mo on the shoulder. "Blow them chunks, Mo. Blow them all."

"Look at this." Reggie pinched something wedged in the bark of a nearby pine.

Black as night, a clump of coarse hair about four inches long spread out from her fingers. More clung to the tree, some wedged in the bark, some in deep cuts running along the side. A few lay higher than any of us stood.

Mo adjusted his glasses, eyes wide. "And that would be what? Was Janet Jackson out here getting nasty with this tree?"

"If by Janet Jackson"—Reggie let the fur free and watched it float away—"you meant 'black bear,' then yes. They rub trees and cut them with their claws to mark territory. Guessing it fed here recently. On whatever that poor thing was."

Something heavy crunched leaves nearby. Followed by another something heavy.

"Very recently," she added.

135

"So, basically we chose to stop in the one spot in the woods that a black bear calls home." Dunk backed toward the creek, eyeing the woods. We followed. "That's fun. Remember when I said we weren't dumb campers? Scratch that."

More crunching. Closer. A snort. A grunt.

"Oh, Lord. Oh, God. Oh, Jesus. I knew I shouldn't have come."

Reggie gripped Mo's arm tight, whispered, "Hush. If we're quiet, it'll—"

"It'll what?" Mo made no effort to follow her lead, as much responding to the bear as the three of us standing beside him. "Eat us slower? Then what? Someone going to fish what's left of us out of its poop to carry *us* to the witch? Or does she draw the line at poopy bits of former humans?"

For the first time since I'd known him, I felt apart from Mo. Too angry with him to think like a friend. "If you just stay quiet, it won't even know we're here!"

"I am not going to stay quiet! What's wrong with all of you? This whole ... escapade is insane nonsense! I'm sorry, Mark," he said, before I could speak, hands waving wildly above his head. "I really am. Your brother was great to me. Always kind. I'm sorry about what happened, but this is madness. Going to a witch with his ashes? Resurrecting him? Please! Look where it's gotten us. We can't go back because Gordon's hunting us. Can't follow the creek because there's a bear waiting to eat us. We're stuck here, if we even survive at all. Stop ... poking ... me ... Reggie!

Unless you have a blow-up raft in that pack of yours, I don't want to hear it."

A louder grunt.

Dunk stepped behind Mo, hand clamped over his mouth, other arm wrapping him tight, pinning his arms at the waist. "Please be quiet now."

Mo fought to break free, but Dunk used the hand over his mouth to force his gaze forward. His eyes widened. He screamed a muffled scream behind Dunk's hand, breath escaping fast from his nostrils. Reggie pressed into me, forced me closer to Mo and Dunk. We backed into the overflow of the creek.

A black bear waddled into the opening, muzzle down, grunting as if having a conversation with itself. It gave a hearty sniff of the kill zone, a few feathers briefly clinging to its snout, then looked up.

I don't think it was shocked to see us. Would have been hard to miss all the yelling and smells of sweaty stinky humans, sugary treats, and juice. But it didn't charge. It just watched us, front half swaying slightly back and forth. Like it was sizing us up. Trying to figure out how to reach us. Maybe to figure out which one of us to eat first, or if it could just eat us all at once.

Mitch talked a lot about bears. I wished I'd listened better. All I could remember was that you had to show the bear you weren't intimidated. If you came off weak, it knew it could win. If you looked like a tough fight, it might give it a second thought. Especially if you had the numbers.

So, despite my instincts to just drop to the ground and wait it out, I raised the Easton in the air, doing my best to shout when my voice wanted to whisper. "Go away!"

Then things happened pretty fast.

First off, the bear wasn't impressed. It stood on its back haunches, taller than any of us by a foot, front paws raised even with its head, long sharp claws extended like black daggers. The sound it produced went beyond a grunt, a warning, or even a growl. It was a war cry. A scream. A notice that things were about to get messy.

We screamed louder.

Reggie grabbed my arm to lower the bat, but knocked it from my hand, barrel landing hard on my shoulder. Despite the searing pain, I tried to catch the Easton, but missed badly. From there it dropped square on Mo's foot. His scream turned, rose into a wail like a banshee and he bit down on Dunk's finger. Dunk let go, swore loudly, shook his hand, and did what any sane person would do after someone bit them. He backed away.

Where his foot landed, there was only water.

When he fell, he still had Mo by the waist.

As his weight shifted Mo grabbed my pack for balance.

Reggie still had my arm.

We dropped into the rapid flow of Edgewater Creek and the world moved in wet, quick blurs, with little air in between.

16

When I was eight, Gordon tried to drown me. The community pool lifeguard—Jake something, I think—didn't see it. He'd just started working his charm on a pair of teen girls seated behind him. Gordon pointed it out to me, insisting I "see how a pro does it." I guess Jake had a bit of a reputation for charm. Even though we were in the shallow end, my toes barely touched bottom. It took all I had just to turn without losing feel of the concrete floor.

The moment my back was to him, he planted both hands on top of my head and pushed down. Once or twice, he let me bob to the surface, for a split second of air, before pushing me back down. I could hear his cackle each time. Not sure why he found it so amusing to watch me flail and gasp for air.

I'd been underwater plenty. Always left the pool with bloodshot eyes that would sting the rest of the day, my vision cloudy but my soul filled by the fun I'd had acting like a shark. Until that moment, the thought of being a water-dwelling boy had always appealed to me. But there, with all the force of his strength holding me down, the world beneath the water suddenly felt as much fun as lying on a bed of knives.

I tried to grip his arms, to force my way free, but he was too strong, even back then. All it amounted to was flailing limbs and splashing water. It shifted me enough to drop a foot closer to the deep end. Best I could manage was to scrape my toes on the floor when he pushed me down. My chest hurt. Against the pressure, I tried to scream, letting fly bubbles of all the air I had in me. Instinctively, I tried to breath, which earned me a mouthful of chlorinated water that I immediately swallowed.

It felt like an hour passed before Mitch pulled me free. He'd been on the other side of the pool, having his own playtime talk with Traci, who he'd just met in class that day. His hands at my underarms, lifting me above the surface, felt like God Himself raising me from beyond. Mitch was yelling, but between my ears being clogged, and coughing so much I thought my lungs might come out, I couldn't hear what he said. We were free of the scores of lounging people—none of whom seemed bothered enough to step in to save me, but sure loved gawking at my struggle—near the bathroom when I threw up the first time.

Mitch waited it out. Let me heave and cry and rid myself of a gallon of water before he placed a hand on my back and gave me his towel.

I'd never seen him so mad.

"What the hell, Gordon?" he yelled, though I have no idea where our cousin was at that point. "Dammit, Mark. Don't let him do that to you. You gotta fight back. Like that girlfriend of yours. She about scratched his eyes out when he grabbed her hair, remember?"

The memory of Reggie slicing Gordon's cheek with her fingernails gave me a boost enough to laugh. But the movement only made me sick again. Once it'd passed and I'd wiped my mouth, I rested against the cool brick wall. "Gross, Mitch. She's not my girlfriend."

"Hey,"—his hands shot up—"don't think I mean that as a bad thing. You got time, though. Maybe by middle school you'll feel different. I know I do." Despite everything, he shot a glance at Traci. Then a smile at me.

"Come on. Let's get home. I'll talk Mama into hitting the Dairy Queen."

I grabbed his hand, my fingers tight around his, and let him take the brunt of the work to get me to my feet. Almost immediately, my balance gave way and the world spun a bit. Then he had me by the shoulders, eyes level to mine, and it passed.

"Thanks," I said, unable to hide the embarrassment of it all.

"For what?"

I nodded toward the pool but didn't look. Didn't want to chance seeing Gordon's grin. "For saving me. For making Gordon let me go."

Mitch laughed. Not the full laugh I loved so much that came straight from his belly and flushed his face. Just simple. Sort of forgiving. "That's what brothers do, man. You and me, right? There for one another to the end."

I didn't swim again for almost a year. Wouldn't even get near the pool if Gordon was within a hundred yards of it.

Most of the memories of the experience faded over time, but I never forgot what it felt like to fight for air that wasn't there. Never forgot the feeling of desperation, the feeling I'd never breathe again, the helplessness of being held underwater, unable to break free. For several hours after, my lungs burned, my throat raw from screaming bubbles, ribs sore. I threw up twice more. Out of nowhere, I'd find myself suddenly gasping like a fish out of water, like there wasn't enough air to make me whole again, fighting a panic I couldn't begin to settle.

Gordon said later it was just a joke.

Never seemed funny to me.

It was horrible. Scary.

Falling into Edgewater Creek was a hundred times worse.

17

The moment I hit the water, I was sucked under, ripped free of Reggie's grip. My knees slammed against the rocky bottom, bolts of pain biting like a thousand needles. The swift water twirled me about feet first, pushed me briefly to the surface, then pulled me under again. The pack dragged beneath me, almost jerked free from my shoulders, but enough to slow me down so I could plant my feet. As I slowed, the force of the creek pressed into my back and pushed me forward, almost upright. A lung full of air gave me a ray of hope, vision clearing long enough to catch sight of Dunk brought to a sudden stop ahead. To hear Mo and Reggie somewhere behind. Then I fell forward, shooting headfirst like a torpedo with Dunk's blue pack and backside as a target.

Much like I had that day in the pool, I flailed with my arms, searching for anything to pull me above water. For any way to bring the torture to an end. I clipped something—or someone; it was hard to tell—and turned sideways, finding the surface once more. I gasped, blinked wildly against watery eyes, and slammed to a stop so hard into Dunk that I could swear every one of my ribs broke. The contents of his pack gave under the impact, the snacks within crushed flat. Crumbs spilled out, drawn away by the current.

Despite the pressure of the water, despite it calling for me to give up my grip on Dunk, I reached around for my pack. To make sure the box was still there. But something slammed into me before my hand got close. Blasted me hard enough to pin me into Dunk. Waves of pain flared along my ribcage, and again I lost my breath. The something behind me coughed in my ear, almost wretched. A soggy braid of black hair whipped in the water over my shoulder. Reggie called my name. Her hands wrapped me tight.

To our right, whooshing by in a blur of arms and legs, Mo screamed, voice trailing like the horn of a passing car. I couldn't understand what he said for the rush of water. It was like being inside a blender. Then he was gone. Out of sight. I managed a hand to my face, wiped the water out of my eyes. Saw Dunk, head barely turned my way, cheeks hot, hair clinging to his forehead. I couldn't make out what he said. His face scrunched and he shouted, eyes clamped shut for a second or two, finger directing my gaze downstream. "Pine! Mo!"

My heart gave another leap. The pine further downstream stretched across the creek, roots ripped out at the base on the bank opposite where we had been. It lay across the rapid flow of water, with no visible gap at all. And Mo was speeding straight toward it.

He must have noticed, because he straightened, rigid as a board, shoes elevated as much as he could. He could have been any other piece of debris in the creek. Granted, one that screamed bloody murder the whole way.

When his feet hit the tree, his knees buckled, body compressed like a spring. For a moment, it looked as though he would hang on. Then his shoes gave against the loosened bark, and he was sucked under the tree. Last thing I saw was his arms pulled free of his pack. One strap caught on a small nub where a branch used to be, the pack bouncing underneath the smallest gap between the trunk and water. The pine made it impossible to tell for sure, but there was no sign of him anywhere.

I tried to call his name, but my sore ribs and the force of Reggie at my back wouldn't allow it. I'd been mad at him. Mad enough to want to slug him. And the last words we'd exchanged were heated. He had to still be there. Had to be.

Despite two bodies and the force of the water pressed into him, Dunk shifted, his arms locking tighter around the trunk of one of the two small trees on the island. He anchored his feet into the rocks on the creek bed and pushed us back. Sometimes I really underestimated how strong he was.

"Tree!" he shouted, nodding to the thin fallen trunk bobbing on the surface to our right. He tried to reach for it, but, as he did, we were nearly pulled back into the rapids.

"You try!"

Not sure what I was supposed to do with it even if I managed to grab hold, I followed his lead. I was pinned against him like the hand of a clock pointing to two, which at least gave me better reach. With Reggie holding me in place from behind, I wasn't going anywhere. Not as long as Dunk held on.

The trunk was slippery. Coated with moss and algae. First few grabs, my fingers just slipped off. It was a good ten feet long, but only about three inches wide. Not too thick, but thick enough to make gripping it with one hand impossible. I adjusted, pulling forward a few more inches, then reached again. I got one hand on the trunk, below the waterline a foot or two from where it broke at the base. Found a grip where a branch had broken, like a small handle. I tried to reach the trunk with my other hand, but I couldn't get my arm fully around Dunk. I didn't have the balance to stick myself out any further.

"Don't move!" Reggie yelled in my ear. Her left hand released me, slapping at Dunk's shoulder until she found his pack. Her weight released a bit and she moved. One more pull on Dunk and then she was off me completely, almost to Dunk's left side, reaching for the second tree to hold her in place. Without her there to block it, the rush of water against my back almost ripped me free, but I was able to use Reggie as a brace to hold my legs. She said something to Dunk, but he couldn't hear her, so she slapped his right hand with her right, pointed to the trunk I held, then back to tree she held. He nodded.

With her left arm wrapped around a tree, Reggie looped her right arm into his left, moved both hands firm alongside his left hand. She dug into the rocky floor of the creek with her feet, then nodded. Secured by Reggie, Dunk shifted, able to reach the bobbing trunk. He leaned into it, cradling the trunk in the crook of his arm.

He was close enough to me now that I heard him clearly. "On three, right? Pull toward Reggie. Don't lift." When I gave him a nod, he counted. On three we pulled. The trunk moved, exposing the break from the base. A single thin strip of bark and pulp held it in place. It was a wonder it hadn't already broken free.

With each pull, the strip lengthened, pulp ripping away, until it had nothing left to hold. The tree almost cut loose of our grip, but Reggie found the branch handle and pulled. Dunk led the trunk, threading it between the island rocks and two remaining trees until the force of the flowing water added the pressure needed to hold it in place. When he was sure it was secure, he pointed to what remained of the top of the trunk.

"Only a few feet from the bank," he shouted. "Feet down. Use it like a rope. I'll hold on. You two go first."

Water splayed over the top of the trunk. It wobbled but seemed stable. I had no desire to be the guinea pig, but I also had no desire to stay where we were. At some point we'd tire and lose our grip. Then the creek could wash us wherever it wanted. Wherever it took Mo.

The moment I reached for it, though, the creek seized me by the waist and nearly took me underneath. Dunk snatched a strap of my pack, held on until I found a good grip on the trunk. Then he gave me a thumbs up. "It'll be fine! Just hold tight!"

Once I had my feet planted, hands gripped tight around the trunk, I was able to stand. Though it had seemed before like the water was as deep as a river, it barely reached my shoulders. The force of the rapids pressed into me like a crowd of hands, squeezing me tight against the trunk as I slowly moved. What remained of the top of the trunk was far thinner and it gave a bit as I moved along. Bent like a bow drawing an arrow. The bank curved outward, the creek pooling along the rim in tiny swirls, the pull of the water far less. Despite the worry screaming in my head, I released the trunk and let the slower flow of water guide my clumsy steps to the bank. I found a firm grip on the roots of a tree and pulled myself out of the water.

By the time I turned, Reggie had already made her way over. I tossed my pack aside to help her up. Dunk followed but needed some assistance to reach the bank. Immediately, he rolled over, hands to his left ankle. He didn't even give me a chance to ask.

"See if you can see Mo! I'll wait here!"

There was a moment—a few seconds that felt like an eternity—when I stared at my pack. Safely on the bank, the fear kicked in. The water. Reggie's collision into my back. If the bag busted, what would I find?

"Go! I'll check it!"

Reggie took off while I stared at my pack, heart hammering. What if ... what if ... what if ....

But the shrill call of Mo's scream pulled me free. From somewhere on the other side of the pine. If he was still there, we could try to save him before the water washed him down the creek.

From my vantage on the bank, I could just make him out. He held on by one of the straps of his pack near the base of the tree, body swaying and bouncing in the water like a motorboat at high speed. His glasses were gone. Every scream took with it a mouthful of water.

Getting to the tree was difficult. The bank was thick with brambles and shrubs. Reggie tried to push them away with a fallen limb, but it didn't give us enough room.

"We'll have to go around."

She was off before I could stop her. I didn't follow. The trunk of the tree went straight into the heart of the brambles. It'd be no easier from the other side. It didn't look like Mo could hold on much longer. Like me, he wasn't a strong kid. Weak didn't even cover it for either of us. There was only one way to get to him. And I wasn't going to sit around debating it.

Mitch certainly wouldn't have.

Mo needed me.

I dropped on my butt, inching my way right up against the bushy obstruction. The water pulled at my feet, but not too bad. I was able to slide into the water and creep along the bank to the trunk without getting sucked into the rapids. From somewhere beyond the brambles I heard Reggie call my name.

The segmented bark of the pine was as slippery as a freshly mopped floor. Getting a good grip was near impossible. It was too wide to hug and, as I creeped out, the pull of the water threatened to pull me under the trunk as it had Mo. He yelled again, but I couldn't see him anymore. Still, I knew he was there, on the other side of the tree, and that drove me on.

I went as far as I could. Until the water started to latch onto me. Then I pulled myself up as far as I could, swung a leg a few times until it looped over the trunk—with everything short of grace. Finally, though, I got my foot high enough to land it on the opposite side and locked in place. With the little bit of security it offered, I was able to pull myself up. I hugged that tree as hard as I could, making no movement at all. Sure any second I'd fall and that'd be the end of me.

Every muscle and bone in my ribcage throbbed and burned. My knees hurt. Showed some blood that thinned in my water-logged jeans. The pine's bark, slippery though it was, still pricked at my hand and fingers. But I found a steady hold and managed to inch forward. Mo was only a few feet away. His eyes were wide and desperate. I knew he couldn't see me clearly, so I called out to him as I crawled along the trunk like a caterpillar, rubbing my thighs raw.

The splintered limb his pack had caught held it well. It wasn't going anywhere. Especially as long as Moe held it taut from the other side of the trunk. My best chance was to grab hold of the strap looped on the front side and hope I could reach him on the back without us both getting sucked away. But he wasn't close enough for me to reach. I dropped my left foot into the water and let the creek push it underneath the trunk. When I felt my hand on the hooked strap and foot underneath were as secure as could be, I reached out for Mo. Still not close enough.

"Give me your hand!"

Mo shook his head. He had both hands on the strap. Tight. Unrelenting. As if it were all that kept him alive. The seam had torn a quarter of the way, exposed thread widening a small gap to about halfway down. It wouldn't hold much longer.

I waggled my fingers at him, stretching as far as I could without dropping. "Come on! I can't reach you!"

Mo started to speak but water filled his mouth. He spat it out. The seam ripped further. It was enough for him to decide he'd had enough of the creek. His right hand slapped at air, grazing my fingertips. When it fell, it splashed into the creek, but found the base of the pack underneath the trunk. He gripped tight and managed to pull himself up a few more inches, then took a long look at me. After a few checks of his grip on the base of the pack, his left hand let go of the strap and he launched it into mine. We slapped at each other a few times before we found a grip tight enough. I wouldn't be able to hold him long. Hoping to find some leverage, I rolled toward him best I could, leg wrapping tighter against the trunk. Mo fished for a grip on the trunk until he found one that worked. Once more, I leaned away, now as far as I could go without toppling over, and pulled with everything I had.

With both hands over the top of the trunk, I was able to help him pull himself up far enough to be free of the water. Mo was far more limber than any of us. More than once he'd proven it by doing splits that made Dunk and I squeamish. With his chest now against the trunk, he swung a leg up and over. Quicker than a cat clawing out of a tub, he was on the trunk beside me.

"Backward," I said, nodding toward the pooled water by the bank. "The water isn't bad over there."

With only a nod, he slinked back along the trunk, following my lead.

By the time we hit the water, Reggie had a heavy fallen branch waiting for us to grab. She helped each of us up, and we collapsed on the ground, breath coming heavy like we'd never have enough air again. After a few seconds, Mo swiveled his head to the side, squinting in my direction.

"This is why the only Olympic events that matter are gymnastics and ice skating. Water sports are way overrated." Mo broke into a wide smile, his teeth bright, cheeks beaded with water. Then he laughed. A giggle that grew until his entire body bounced. Reggie sat beside us, laughing as well.

Mitch once told me that even in the darkest of places, laughter brings light. In that moment, I had no idea what was so funny. We had almost died. But I couldn't stop myself. I laughed until the horror of the past few minutes faded. I laughed until the hurt in my ribs forced me to stop. Then I remembered why we were out there at all.

As if lifted by the thought, I hopped to my feet and ran to my pack.

What I found turned my stomach.

18

Dunk sat on the wet ground, grassy spots sprouting here and there around his extended legs, his back pressed into the trunk of a wide oak several feet from the creek. Off to the side, his pack lay open. Scrunched and crumbled Pop Tarts and smushed snack cakes littered the ground, packages busted open. His shoe was off, soggy and pulled away from the sole around the heel, wet tube sock tossed aside and curled like an odd-looking white snake with red and blue stripes around its tail. His ankle and foot were swollen twice the normal size, reddened skin tinged in a purplish haze.

It was bad. Maybe broken.

My pack lay between his knees, sodden shoe-box creased deep where it had been squished like an accordion when Reggie slammed into me. The bag was visible through the open top, seemingly fine, still closed, all contents within as dry as could be.

All of which paled in comparison to the sight of Gordon's gun stretched across Dunk's open palms. He held it like a bomb, like some terrible thing about to strike, his eyes set on me. Accusatory and disappointed. "It fell out when I got the box," he said, tone even, almost a whisper.

Mo squinted around my shoulder. "What's that?"

Before Reggie even spoke, a part of my attention drifted to her, expectant. Awaiting the inevitable. The best I could do was cut my eyes to her at my side. I couldn't bring myself to look at her fully.

"Why does Dunk have a gun?" Then, before I could respond, "Dunk has a gun, Mark. He has your pack, the ashes, and a gun. *Why does he have a gun?*" The last rose to a shriek. I flinched, just as when Mama's voice got firm. It wasn't out of fear of a strike. It was purely out of fear that my soul would jump free, unwilling to stick around for the worst of it, unwilling to come back to check on me.

"I—" There was no good answer. No lie that would satisfy the moment. Fresh from the creek, my friends still in one piece, I couldn't find a single reason to deny them the only truth I had. "I don't know. Really. I mean, I know why he has it. I just don't know why I put it in my pack."

"You don't know why? How can you not … Forget that," said Reggie, hands waving wildly as she stepped between me and Dunk, her nose a foot from mine, dark eyes burning hotter than coal ever could. It was only then that I realized her cap was gone, her pack nowhere in sight. Probably down the creek and past town at this point. Her hair was drenched, some black strands clinging to her neck, freed from braids that fell over her shoulders. "*How* did you even get a gun?"

I shrugged, not intending it as an answer. More of a kickstart to the words in my head. "Gordon's car. Under the seat. The lace holding the card—" My heart skipped a beat as the image of the card flashed in my head, my hands fumbling around the collar of my shirt until they found the shoelace. With everything that had happened, I had totally forgotten about it. Fortunately, it was there, the card still attached. The plastic holder was airtight, so the beaming face of Dale Murphy was still unblemished. I exhaled, at peace for a second. Until I took a quick mental inventory.

Ashes, check.

Card, check.

Easton …

Without a word, I shot by Reggie's shoulder, scrambling further up the creek, opposite the spot where we'd fallen. I scanned across the water, along the bank. It was clear. No sign of the bear. No bat in sight. "I had it. It dropped. We fell. It has to be there. Has to be."

Reggie was on my heels, holding firm to the matter of the gun. "You found a gun in his car and took it? What on earth for? Were you planning on using it? Hello? What are you mumbling about?"

"Bat," I said, hands twisting about one another, tight enough to turn my knuckles white. "I had it, but dropped it when … I don't see it. It has to still be there. Do you see it?"

"Mark, this is serious. You have a gun—"

"Do you see it?" The words burned my throat as I shouted, somehow louder than the roar of the creek, louder than the bear, louder than God. Something bit at my throat. Fell into my chest. My eyes burned.

Reggie held silent a few seconds. Finally, she stepped alongside me, side of her hand planted across her eyebrows like it somehow turned her vision into a superpower. "No. Nowhere."

"It hit my foot," said Mo, from somewhere behind me. His voice came soft. Almost apologetic. "I think it went in when we did."

I knew he was right, but I shook my head anyway. It couldn't be true. It just couldn't. But the truth was plain. Whether I wanted to believe it or not. If the bat was on the bank, we'd see it. There'd be some flash of dull silver telling me it was fine. But it was gone. Mitch's Easton was gone.

The Mall.

The map.

Zippy.

Now the Easton.

Mitch never had a problem sharing his things with me. His only rule was to respect what it meant to him and to bring it back in one piece. I'd failed him four times already and we hadn't even reached the witch. The weight of it filled my head like a mountain's worth of rocks.

What if I failed him there too?

The something inside me lurched.

I swallowed hard and pushed it back.

Reggie's hand on my shoulder knocked the thought free. She turned me to face her. I had to look away. Away from her. Away from the water. Away from the realization I'd never find the Easton. "I'm sorry about the bat. Really. But the gun, Mark. We need to get rid of the gun."

"No!" I rushed back to Dunk and snatched the gun from his palms, hand tight to the grip, pointer finger curled away from the trigger, barrel aimed at the ground. "I need it. It's his. He always talked about it like it was some kind of pet. It meant something to him. I can give it to her if the card isn't enough."

The gun shook in my hand. I locked my other around it. It didn't help.

"Is that why he's chasing us?" Dunk spoke through gritted teeth. Pain laced every single word.

I didn't need to consider it. "Yeah, I think so."

"Well, that's a first," snorted Mo, drawing our attention. "What? No, really. What? Your faces are hard to see. I assume you're glaring at me like I've cursed the Almighty, but it's true, Mark. When have you really thought about any of this? You saved me out there. And for that, you have my eternal forgiveness for all the wrongs you're bound to commit. But you haven't thought much about anything since we started this insane trip, or about how it affects any of us."

"I did so. I thought so from the moment I heard the news."

Mo shrugged. "Sure. Okay. You *thought* about it in that moment. I often *think* about being a touring dancer for Madonna. But that's a goal, not a plan. It's not even a good goal. I mean, look at me. So, I have to plan on being some twittering nitwit weakling being poked fun at for wanting to dance when I'm barely built to bag groceries."

"So?"

"*So*," said Mo, eyes rolling as he landed heavily on the word, "thinking about what I want, and opening a door to see what it looks like doesn't make it a reality. Any more than you deciding to steal those ashes. But it isn't just you. You aren't the only one out here, trying to get to the witch. We're here with you. Everything you do affects us, and we've been affected more on this trip than any of us bargained for."

I stared at him, passed a look over them all. "You didn't have to agree to come."

"Dude," said Dunk, "you asked us to. Of course we're going to say yes."

My gaze found my feet. My shoes were damp, muddy around the base. Between the rips and blood, my jeans and t-shirt were near ruined. Mama wasn't going to like it. I hadn't planned on that either. "You could have said no."

"You said you needed us," said Reggie. I couldn't remember her face ever looking as it did. Serious, but with a softness I couldn't look away from. "You *do* need us. You can't go there alone."

Mo drew even with me, cautious, arms outward and eyes almost squinted shut as he tried to see the gun, to make sure it pointed down. He patted my cheek. "Silly child. No way we would have said no. No way. Friends don't abandon each other, whether they're at war with a creek or dealing with something like this. We don't have to agree. It'd be boring if we did. Better or worse, we're in it together, whatever *it* is. You needed us and we're here. But please, for the love of all things holy and sacred, stop and think about what *we're* doing next? I don't have the stamina to almost die more than once a day, and we're well past that. Now, would you put the damn gun down so I can hug you?"

The *something* returned. Packed a hell of a wallop. Made it into my throat before I managed to steer it away. Muscles in my face tightened, then relaxed. Somehow, I managed a laugh. Nodded, then set the gun at my feet. Before I could get upright, Mo and Reggie both launched into me. Nearly bowled me over. The hug didn't last long, but it lifted my spirits.

"I'm sorry," I said, trying to look at them, but doing a horrible job of it. "I'm glad you're all here."

"Good," said Mo, beaming. "I can work with that. Now, put your pack back together and let's finish our witch hunt."

"What about the gun?" Reggie nudged it with the toes of her shoe.

Mo smirked, one brow raised. A look I'd seen a thousand times before. Something between disgust and a need for trouble. "If Mark thinks the witch might want it, then it comes with us. But I swear, if that thing comes out of the pack again, or goes off, the Diva Demon will rise within so fast and furious, not even Indiana Jones will be able to find what's left of you."

Dunk laughed so hard he snorted. "In that case, someone find me a branch or something to use as a crutch. The Diva Demon is my favorite. I'm not missing that."

19

As we searched the nearby woods for a branch we could turn into a crutch for Dunk, he sang his way through a pitchy version of "Manic Monday." Between that and what I suppose were dance moves he made while still on the ground, back to the tree, there wasn't much room for me to focus on the things building in my head.

Dunk never failed to entertain. I can say that for certain.

He broke mid-lyric, drawing our full attention.

"You know, I love this song. Like, *really* love this song. But who takes an airplane to work? I mean, if you know you have to catch an early train, then what's an airplane got to do with it? And who misses a train and says, 'Man, I wish I had a plane,' right? And, if you can't get there on time by plane, then you're just late to begin with. That's not Monday's fault. That's just bad planning."

He didn't wait for answer. Not that one was coming. Listening to him try to impersonate Susanna Hoffs took the edge off everything we'd been through.

I have no idea how he managed the pain enough to sing a song, much less chat casually about it, but I had to admire him for it. I'd been known to burst into tears over a stubbed toe. More than once. Reggie had taken the shoelaces out of her sneakers and braced Dunk's ankle with a branch she broke into two pieces. Had her pack not washed downstream, she said she could have wrapped it with a cloth bandage and kept it steady. But this would have to do.

As I circled a wide maple, I caught a glance from Reggie some distance away, near a few pines. She gave me a quick smile, shook her head as Dunk broke into the chorus, and went back to the search. I wasn't sure where Mo had gone, but I knew he'd stayed close by given he could hardly see.

Dunk broke away from the song again, a daydreamy expression on his face. "Man, you guys, that bit in the video when she's making out with that dude? Multiplies my love for this song by the power of erection."

"Oh, Duncan," sighed Reggie as she dipped behind a cluster of trees.

Mo's groan made it easier to find him. He stood a little behind Dunk, halfway into a thick layer of brush, hands planted on his hips. "That's so gross. Even for you."

"What? It's the call of the wild. Hormonal. We're teens now. Can't be blamed for all these crazy thoughts going through my head. Not like I can control it."

"Not that you want to, you mean," Mo added.

"No way. Why would I? I can't be blamed for the primal need growing inside me. What about y'all? We all got body changes happening. Look at Reggie, she didn't used to have titties and now—"

"No, no, no, no, and no." Mo's voice rose high enough to block out the creek. "No sir."

Reggie snatched a branch from the ground. "This is exactly what my dad was talking about."

"All right, fine. But you can't deny it. We aren't kids anymore. We're hormonal superheroes fighting the villainy of a sex-crazed world."

Mo's head bobbed in a steady shake. "Uh uh. Nope. I decline your opinion."

Dunk's face scrunched, brows joined together like a long hairy caterpillar. Then he smiled, nodded knowingly. "You mean you *disagree* with my opinion?"

"No," snapped Mo. "I just decline it. I don't want to agree with it or disagree with it. I just want it to go away."

Despite everything, I couldn't hold back a laugh. "Burn."

Before Dunk could respond, Reggie planted the branch at her feet and snapped off two forked limbs from the end, making it look like an uneven 'y' drawn by a first grader. It made it nearly up to her arm pits and looked as though it would give Dunk a solid base to lean some weight into.

"You say one more word about my titties and I'll club you upside the head so hard, you won't remember whether you're a boy or a girl."

Dunk nodded, considered the thought. "Always wondered what being a girl was like. Good to know I may find out."

20

The woods along the west bank of the creek were much easier to pass through. No sign of bears or psycho cousins. The ground squished with each step, underneath a thick layer of leaves and grass that kept our shoes from sinking into mud. Reggie had to work carefully without shoelaces to hold her sneakers tight. They kept trying to pull away with each step through the muck. The overcast skies had lightened, clouds thinning enough to promise some hope we'd eventually see the sun again.

We had no idea what time it was. The creek had killed whatever life remained in Mo's watch. It felt like most of the day had passed just in the time we spent in the creek and trying to find Dunk a crutch. It might have only been a couple of hours since the Junkyard. Might have been much more. Regardless, getting to the witch and back all in one day was starting to seem impossible. Once dark fell, the woods would turn into one great big menacing shadow. A shadow with bears, and who knew what other beasts. Add to that, losing Reggie's pack meant we'd be without her small dome tent, blankets, and hammock.

I wanted to run. To get to the witch before it was too late. But I couldn't. *We* couldn't.

Without his glasses, Mo had to tow along behind me, fingers tucked into an open pouch of my pack. At every splintered tree trunk draped across the path, cluster of prickly branches, or dip in the ground, I had to guide him past. But it was Dunk that really slowed things down.

Without his pack, he had better leverage. Between the ruined food supply and goopy layers of jelly and chocolate cake smushed all over the inside, there wasn't much of his pack to salvage anyway. Even the Uno cards were beyond saving. After eating what we could of the few bits of food that weren't entirely soaked, we'd tossed it into the creek. No need to invite more bears to the party by leaving it behind.

Reggie carried a second branch, in case the first gave way. It only had a nub a quarter of the way down from a split limb, like a three-inch handle. Wasn't comfortable at all for Dunk, but if needed it would do. She twirled and stabbed it through the air like a sword as she went. I decided to add "ninja" to the list of previous lives I felt certain she'd lived.

"On the plus side," Mo said, sleeve of his shirt pinched between fingers, "you're off the hook, Dunk. Looks like the creek washed the jelly from my shirt. Edgewater Creek, one, Tide, zero."

"That's a relief. Been weighing real heavy on my mind."

"Funny guy. You don't appreciate the Goddess the way I do."

Dunk snorted a short laugh. "Not gonna, either. I mean, come on. It's just a shirt. Your love affair with it only gives kids reason to pick on you."

Mo pulled me to a stop so he could face Dunk. "You think my love for Madonna is why I get picked on? Adjust your television set. I think your color's off." He let go of me long enough to sweep both hands from his head down. "There's a whole skin thing going on here that sets me apart, in case you didn't notice. I could wear the flag for a shirt and all this still remains. Ripe for abuse."

"Dude, I'm thinking wearing the flag might not help either. Not unless you want to set the Duke boys off. Pretty sure they'd just drive General Lee through your house and call it a day."

With enough force to bend me at the knee, Mo latched onto my pack and pushed me on.

"Bunch of undignified morons. You should know better, Dunk."

"Aw, come on, Mo!" Dunk said, the sharp smack of his gut giving me a start. "We've all got our issues. Look at me. I make Jabba the Hut look like Iman. I'm just ribbing you. Doesn't matter what anyone says—and honestly, they need to deal with me if they have a problem with you—there isn't anyone alive with a voice like yours. When you sang 'O Holy Night' at the school Christmas dealy last year? Gave me chills. Legit, dude. And everyone stood for you. I don't think they gave a rat's ass right then what color you are. For the record, I sure as hell don't."

Reggie gave Mo a simple nod, lips turned up at the corner. "It was beautiful."

"Totally," I added, without turning away from the woods ahead.

Mo sniffed. He wasn't crying. I didn't need to look to make sure. It was just the thing he did after we'd thrown him a compliment. Like he needed a second to find his Nice Voice, or something. "Thank you, Duncan. All of you. I appreciate that."

After that, we didn't talk much. Just walked. For a while it was fine. Then it occurred to me we were closing in on Highway 100. Closing in on reaching Spook Hill. Closing in on finding the witch. Which gave me a nice boost for a second or two. Unfortunately, my head followed almost immediately with the burning need to pester me into remembering the last thing Mitch said to me before he left that night to go out with Gordon. Why even think such a thing? What was the point? I didn't want to remember it. Any more than I needed to remember what he said at dinner the Tuesday before. What did it matter what he said if there would be more talks in the future?

Because there might not be. It might have been the last thing he ever said to you, and you don't remember it.

You saved Mo. But what if you can't save Mitch?

What if Officer John was right? What if gone is gone?

Thoughts dropped in my head like atom bombs. No amount of squinting, head shakes, or calls for favorite songs could silence them. Or undo the damage they caused.

Officer John was wrong. Mitch wasn't gone. I'd make sure of it.

Because there had to be more talks. There had to be more memories.

Maybe you should have listened better. Took time to soak up every word.

I always listened! I just couldn't always remember.

You should have tried harder. Now you'll never…

He was coming back! Just like Zippy!

Zippy died. Zippy died and was resurrected by the witch.

So did Mitch. And maybe she can't bring him back. Maybe it's been too long. Maybe she isn't a witch at all. Maybe Mitch lied to you. Maybe dead is dead.

A stitch flared in my chest. My throat tightened. My steps quickened. Mo nearly tumbled behind me.

"He'll be back too," I said, just above a whisper, hoping to silence the evil thoughts once and for all. "Everything will be fine. Everything will be fine."

Right. Exactly. Fine.

The tightness faded. I could breathe easier.

Soon, I wouldn't have to sleep in our room by myself. Soon, Mama could stop drinking her sadness away. Soon she'd buy Mitch a new bat and he could teach me how to hit again. I'd learn fast this time. I'd be great. For him. I'd tell everyone he was the reason I'd become the best hitter the game had ever seen. And he'd be there with me. Both of us playing in the Big Leagues. The Murphy brothers, on their way to Hall of Fame greatness.

"Hey, Murph."

We'd have dinners together and laugh, just like always, as Mitch told bad jokes and Mama playfully scolded him. We'd have donuts every Saturday and watch television each night as a family.

Not as it was. Better this time. Because we'd learned our lesson. We'd learned to value every day, every moment, every word.

We'd learned that having each other around was something to cherish, even in the hard times.

Something tugged at my pack.

"Murph?"

Mitch and I could work on plans for a new Mall. One bigger and better. One we could both sleep over in. Mama would be so pleased with me for bringing him home that she'd be more willing to let me stay out.

Another tug. Harder this time.

Everything would be fine. Better than before.

"Mark!"

Dunk's voice carried through the trees like gunshot. Mo jerked at my pack so hard I almost fell backward. I gathered my footing and faced my friends, distant images of my future with Mitch fading against the backdrop of trees.

For a moment, I wasn't even sure where I was. "What?"

"That." Dunk raised the crutch, hobbling on one foot. I followed where it pointed. Through the trees ahead. To the road some ways off. To the slightest flash of blue light above a stretch of white.

"Officer John."

"How do you know?" Reggie's voice was close. Near my shoulder. I almost grabbed her hand. I don't know why, exactly, but it took a bit of doing to pull back. I buried my hand in a pocket to be safe.

"Has to be. He knows about the witch." When I looked back, they were all staring, mouths open. As expected. I shrugged. "He said so at the Junkyard. Said he's the one who told Mitch about it."

"And you didn't think that tiny little tidbit important enough to tell us?" said Mo.

A sigh dropped from me like a lead weight. "Can we please just call this one of those 'Mark was only thinking about himself on this trip' things and move on? I'm sorry I didn't mention it."

The lights spun. We were still too far off for him to have seen us. As it was, only the top half of his car was visible. If I'd matched a Hot Wheel against it, they'd have been the same size.

"Didn't think he'd be out here waiting. He just told me not to go. To take the ashes home."

Reggie slid beside me, shoulder to mine, peering through the trees. "Fine. So we go around, right?"

I tried to see the map in my head. The overpass leading Hwy 100 around the small mountain. The road splintering off toward the "X" of the witch's house. Not that it mattered. Officer John wouldn't worry about splitting the distance. "I don't think so. He's not parked at the overpass. Creek turned back toward the other side a while ago. Can't see it from here. It isn't as loud. If he came out to stop me, then he's parked at the road."

"So, that's it? We give up? After everything we've been through?" I had to appreciate the disappointment in Mo's voice.

"We could wait him out," said Reggie. "He has to give up at some point, right?"

"He won't." And I knew why. It wasn't because of the witch. It wasn't because he thought bringing Mitch back was a bad idea. It wasn't even about me, exactly. "He's doing it for Mama. Can't hate him for it, can I? He's doing right by her. But so am I."

I gave the woods a scan, thinking.

"We can try going further away from the creek. Maybe find 100 up a ways, then cut back through the woods on Spook Hill until we find her road. He won't see us. Doubt he'd even be expecting us from this side of the creek."

Reggie crossed her arms, lips pressed tight, eyes cut. Tell-tale sign she didn't agree. "If he's waiting on us, then he'll be listening for any sign we're coming or got around. Not like walking through the woods is a quiet job. Besides, climbing the slope on wet ground isn't going to be easy." She gave a quick nod to Dunk. "He can barely walk as it is. Sorry, Dunk."

Dunk gave a thumbs up. "Right there with you, sister. I don't care for climbing things even with two good ankles."

I measured my response, eyeing them all. "Then I'll go by myself."

"Like hell you will," fired Mo. When I didn't respond, he nudged Reggie. "What's his expression? I want to believe it's all soft and contrite, full of honor and love for my defiance."

"It isn't," said Reggie.

"Ah, well. So much for breaking out into 'Thank you for being a friend.'"

I turned away. Eyed the blue lights. Scanned the woods. There had to be a way. I had to make it to the witch. It was already early afternoon. It couldn't wait any longer.

"Murph? Hey, Murphy. Jesus Christ, Mary, and Murph!"

Something solid clocked the bone of my ankle. "Ow!"

Dunk smiled at me. Nudged me in the butt more gently with his crutch. "Sorry. Maybe next time don't make me say your name three times or go all sacrilegious in front of Mo before you respond, and I won't feel like I have to cause you pain to get your attention. Now, move out of the way. Fatty needs room. I have an idea. But you won't like it."

21

Mitch covered for Gordon once, back when I was a newbie in sixth grade. Took the blame for tripping a kid in the hall even though he was standing next to me and Mo about ten feet away.

The kid, Trevor White, was in my grade. Had braces, wild red hair that always looked like a ball of yarn had exploded, face covered by so many freckles an army of red ants would have feared them, had bad asthma, and never made less than an A on anything. Ever.

He made us look cool by comparison.

When he fell, he had an armful of books and notebooks. They went flying everywhere, loose paper spread all over the hall. Kids laughed without care for the pain it caused him. Easy to laugh when it isn't you, I suppose. Because Trevor's books were as much best friends as they were shield and armor, he'd tried to protect them. He didn't brace for the fall at all. Hit the tile floor elbows first. Cracked the bone in each. Wound up with casts on both arms for the next two months.

Like he needed some other reason for kids to poke fun at him.

Gordon was already in deep with the principal for fighting. If he stepped out of line again, he'd be expelled. Mitch rushed to Trevor and tried to help him up, but that only made it worse. When Trevor's screams started, teachers flooded the hallway. Mitch wasted no time, assuring them all he was the one who tripped Trevor. It was an accident, he said, and he felt horrible for it. He'd just turned at the wrong time.

Fortunately for Gordon, no one fessed up to seeing him do it. Trevor sure didn't know. He always walked with his eyes to the floor. A foot was a foot from that angle. The teachers, on the other hand, seemed sure Gordon had something to do with it. But he played his part well. As if it had been rehearsed, he played off Mitch's story like there couldn't be another truth so certain in the entire universe.

Mitch didn't get in trouble. No one would ever think him the type to hurt a kid for no reason.

On the way home, I asked him why he'd done it.

"Because friendship isn't about using common sense," he said, then refused to say anything more. But he never took the fall for Gordon again.

If I needed assurance Dunk agreed with Mitch's definition, he'd given it.

"I don't like it," I said, crossing my arms as if that brought an end to the discussion.

"Told ya." Dunk eyed Mo and Reggie and bounced a thumb my way. "For my next prediction, Dunk the Wise sees himself doing it anyway."

"It's a stupid plan," I said under my breath, as heated as I'd felt since the incident with Mo earlier. "What happened to being in this together? You can't just give yourself up."

"Sure I can. I just walk up to ole Offy Johnny and tell him you all washed down the creek and that I went all Hulk to pull myself free and wandered this way because I'm young, dumb, and hobbling on an elephant foot. And oh, by the way, psycho Gordo is trying to kill us. Help, help and stuff."

"I won't let you."

Dunk laughed so hard he snorted. Then he slapped his gut. "Even on one leg I could demolish you like a delicious syrupy pancake. I mean, you're my bud and all, Murph, but you're as short as that Hobbit guy from that book you like so much."

"You mean *The Hobbit*?"

"That what it's called? Man. More books oughta be so easy to remember."

At my pleading glance, Mo and Reggie shifted beside Dunk.

"He's right," Reggie said. "He's giving us a chance to get past. And he needs a doctor."

I held firm. "It isn't going to work. He'll just put Dunk in the backseat and wait."

Dunk straightened on his makeshift crutch, edging a step my way. "No problemo. I'm damn hungry right now, so I've got what I need to work with. I'll fall to the ground and scream about the pain. He's an adult, responsible and shit. He'll take me back to town. Trust me. I'm a great dramaturd."

"It's *dramaturge*. Simpletons," said Mo with a pointed sigh and eye roll. "And you aren't even using it ... You know what? Never mind. Go with that. It works for you."

Before I could carry on with the fight, Dunk tapped my leg with the branch. "Look, I'd rather go with you to the witch. I would. But we all know I'd just slow you down. If I could make it up that hill at all. I'm a gimp. And it's only getting worse. There's no way you're getting to her with Johnny Boy standing watch, so we need him to have a reason to leave. This is it."

Reggie latched onto my arm. I pushed her off. She latched on again with both hands and pulled. "We need to hide, Mark. If Officer John sees us, it won't matter what Dunk says."

"We can't just let Dunk get carried back to town in a cop car!" I tried to shake her loose, but her fingers may as well have been handcuffs that needed a key to unlock.

"Oh, stop. He's not being arrested."

I pulled against her weight, leaning like a loose post. "He may as well be."

"Dunk will be—"

"Oh, for the love of everything holy!" Mo tried to pry us apart but had no better luck freeing Reggie's grip than I did. At a loss, he slapped at her arms, beating red welts into the skin until she let go. "Would you two quit your twisted little marital squabble and shut up? Mark, Dunk is doing right by us, and giving you a chance to make it to the witch. You should be grateful for it. And Reggie, girl, I'm beginning to wonder if you have hands or vise grips on the end of those arms. Damn you're strong."

We fell silent. Bird chatter filled the air, as if they agreed with Mo on account of wanting us gone, regardless. The creek roared back to life in the distance.

Finger-sized red lines marked my arm. As the blood flowed, free from the dam of her grip, they vanished. "It's not ... We're not ... marital squabble." A quick glance confirmed Reggie was as interested in the ground as I was. "I'm just worried about Dunk."

"Whatever you need to tell yourself," Mo said, a snap in his tone. "Just don't think you're the only friend out here worrying about another friend."

For a moment, I stumbled over some words that didn't seem to want to work together to form a sentence. Finally, I hitched my pack higher and nodded.

Mo widened his eyes, moved closer, then squinted. "I'm going to assume my unparalleled brilliance and insight have wowed you to the point of agreement. So, can you please lead this blind Einstein somewhere clear of sight, so we don't join Dunk for a less than joyful ride in the Popomobile?"

"Fine." I eyed Dunk but couldn't hold it. I watched the lights of Officer John's car for a few seconds. "Thanks."

Dunk patted my shoulder. "My pleasure, dude. Just do me a favor and let me know what I missed. I've always wanted to know what a real witch looked like. Is she a deformed hag with ratty hair, bulging eyes, and a fat ole wart on her nose? Or does her magic allow her to stay forever young, nice on the eyes, and a temptation to every young man who wanders her way?"

"Nice," said Reggie, though she couldn't contain a smile.

"You know what? Never mind. Don't tell me. I don't want to wreck my fantasies."

Without another word, he turned and hobbled off. It took everything in me not to run after him. As if reading my mind, Reggie shook her head and pointed deeper into the woods to our left.

By the time we settled into a spot behind a fallen tree, Dunk was nearly halfway to the road. He'd taken to humming loudly and shouting "Help, help" without zero enthusiasm for it every few seconds. Finally, a door opened. Officer John stepped out of the car, straightening his hat. The moment he fixed on Dunk, he scrambled into motion, nearly slipping down the muddy wooded embankment to reach him.

It took some doing, one of Dunk's arms looped over his shoulder, but Officer John managed to pull him up to the road. Dunk seemed to be putting on a nice show, the sounds of his moans rising over the creek. After a few seconds of talk, Officer John turned back to the woods, hands to his hips.

He wasn't buying it.

Safe from view though we were, we ducked as low behind the trunk as we could without losing sight of what was happening. Officer John shook his head to something Dunk said. Dunk said something else. Officer John stepped our way.

It was at that point that Dunk collapsed, hands to his foot, wailing in pain. It was excessive, definitely more dramatic than called for, but it did the trick. Officer John backed toward him, giving up on the woods as he knelt to Dunk. A moment later, Dunk was in the back seat. The car wheeled in a slow turn onto the side road shooting up Spook Hill, rolled back, then rushed off down Highway 100, back toward town, spinning lights visible through the trees.

Then they were gone.

The road to the witch was clear.

It was time. Time to carry Mitch to her. Time to bring him back.

The *something* in me rose again and screamed *NO* as loud as it could.

I kind of agreed.

After a few steps in the opposite direction from where we needed to go, I backed into a tree. Slid to the ground, pack clutched tight, the point of the box pressed into my chest.

Suddenly I was in my room again, paralyzed on the floor.

Only this time I wasn't sure I'd ever get up.

22

Reggie leaned into view. Her mouth moved. Over the rush of blood in my ears and the thunderous beat of my heart, I couldn't make out the words. My breath came in heavy waves, tightening my grip on the pack—on the shoebox—with each draw of air. My eyes widened until it felt like they took up most of my head. Then I couldn't breathe at all. I tried to stop it. To stop the pain in my chest. To draw air. But it worsened with each try.

Spots drifted into the light. The woods darkened.

Visions of Mama pressed into my thoughts. The crying. The drinking. The sorrow. She missed Mitch. That much I knew. But how did what I felt compare to her? Her son was gone from her. Her *son*. I'd never really put it into focus. What this meant to her. What *he* meant to her. She needed Mitch back. So she could live again. So she could breathe again.

Breathe.
Breathe.

"Breathe, Mark!"

Something sharp struck my cheek. Reggie's hand. Strangely, there was no pain. Just a ... sensation. Warmth. Then nothing. But my vision cleared a bit. She was there. Saying my name. Her hand rising. Falling. Striking my cheek once more.

This time it hurt. My lungs seized, then opened. Air flooded both, filling, then withdrawing. Again. And again. And again. A deep sting rose in my cheek. It throbbed. Pulsed heavy with my heart. Warmth gave way to numbness. Numbness to intense pain stretching from my jaw to my ear. When I touched it, the skin felt inflamed, puffy, tight.

The pinpricks of darkness faded. The woods returned. Reggie panting, crouching next to me, hands tight on my shoulders, her forehead to mine. Mo hovered behind, his face slack, mouth wide. A sharpness prodded my chest. Like a nail into my ribs. The pack. The shoebox. I uncoiled my arms. Pushed the pack off me like it was a bag of hot coals. Watched it tumble to the ground.

"I can't." The words couldn't have come from me. But it was my voice. As if searching for proof, I touched my lips, lowered my hand to my throat. Made the words my own. "I can't."

"You can't breathe?" Reggie lowered her grip to my arms. Ready to shake the air back into me.

"I can't. I can't." I looked at the pack.

It was enough. Reggie relaxed. Inched back. Sat down in front of me, hands grasping mine. "It's okay. We're here with you."

Every muscle in my throat tightened. The *something* within returned, stronger than ever. I fought it. Tried to swallow it back. I kept my gaze on her hands. Flexed my fingers. Tried to focus on their movements. On sounds. On anything else.

Mo sat beside her. His hands fell atop Reggie's.

I swallowed harder. My eyes burned.

"We'll go together," said Mo.

"We're almost there," said Reggie.

Together.

Almost there.

For Mama.

For Mitch.

For me.

I nodded, as reluctant to do anything as I'd ever been. Latched onto my pack. Accepted their help to my feet without taking my gaze off the forest floor. I took an exaggerated breath, felt my lungs expand, and steadied myself. I wanted to thank them, to tell them how much it meant to me that they were there, but nothing would come. Finally, I tossed the pack over my shoulder and faced away.

"We know," said Reggie, pulling thoughts from my head again like no one else could, her hand grasping my left.

Mo grabbed my right hand.

Then we headed for the road.

Together.

23

ighway 100 was quiet. The smell of wet pavement lay thick. There was no breeze. If not for the rushing waters of Edgewater Creek, all might have felt still. As if the entire world had fallen silent. Waiting on me. The two-lane road hadn't been paved in a long while. Cracks and quarter-sized holes pitted the asphalt. Time had faded the solid yellow lines running along the center to a faint glow.

Across 100, a narrow road wound upward. Rain-washed, the base was more gravel than pavement, marked only by Officer John's tires, clearly unused within the past several hours otherwise.

A rusted silver pole leaned to a side at the corner of the small road and 100, like it was using every ounce of willpower just to stay upright. The crooked sign atop read SPOOK HILL RD, white letters bright against the chipped green backdrop. After a quick glance at Reggie and Mo, we crossed 100 in a line and began the walk up.

Between the wet pavement and patches of gravel, the journey wasn't easy. Mo stumbled a few times, unable to see the rocks clearly. Reggie eventually pulled him alongside, gripped him by the hand and guided his steps.

After the second driveway—which led to small cottage-style home that looked every bit as normal as anything—Reggie broke the silence. "How will we know which one is hers?"

The third driveway was close enough to make out the faded white numbers on the black mailbox. 3683. The house looked more or less the same as the others.

"The map made it seem like it was up a bit. The 'x' was on the left side, I think. Mitch said he knew it the moment he saw it. I can't remember the number though."

Mo made a sound, something like a word falling into a deep breath, but Reggie cut him off with a whispered "Not now," then nothing else was said. I didn't look back.

Whether from the walk, or knowing where the walk led, my heart raced. My legs felt weak, thigh muscles burning. The pack seemed to gain a pound for each driveway we passed. I didn't know how much longer I could walk. I just knew I couldn't stop.

Then we were there.

"This is it. This is where she lives," I said, voice lighter than a breath.

The dented, rusted mailbox bore the numbers 3702. It clicked the moment I saw it. That was what Mitch wrote on the map. But I wouldn't have needed that memory to know I was there. To either side of a gravel drive stood a bear, framed atop a circular cut of pine, five to six feet tall on their back haunches, front paws raised, claws out, ready to strike.

It gave us a start. I think Mo would have screamed if he could have seen them clearly.

But they didn't move.

They couldn't move.

I thought they might have been statues, but the closer we got, the more real they seemed. Once we stood even with the drive, there was no doubt. The fur, the eyes, the teeth, claws; it was all real. One glance down the driveway answered any lingering question.

Coyotes, racoons, squirrels, possums, every type of bird imaginable hanging from tree limbs. The entire path was layered in dead animals. Stuffed, posed, each bearing some manner of threat in their form.

"Holy spooky driveway, Batman." Even without his glasses, the sight was enough to draw Mo's horror.

The driveway went a bit further than the others, bending slightly toward the wooden exterior of an aged cabin. We moved along the drive like Dorothy, the Tin Man, and the Scarecrow walking through the forest. About halfway, beneath a trio of dangling vultures, I came to a stop. The small cabin was layered in ivy, a tiny porch framing a rickety screen door. A lamp sat in a square window, illuminating the interior through white lace drapes. Chimes tinkled in a short breeze.

"Are you all right?"

"No," I said to Reggie, pulling my pack around to my chest. Fighting the urge to drop to the ground again. "Not really."

I unzipped the top, gently took hold of the shoebox and withdrew it. The cardboard wasn't as firm as it had been. My fingers almost dug through the soggy surface. Without much thought, I handed Reggie my pack.

"We can go with you," she said, though I could tell she would have rather chewed her hand off.

I shook my head, swallowed against a sensation like vomit rising into my throat. "I can go alone. I need to."

Reggie nodded, face a blank canvas. "We'll be right here."

My mouth opened. Closed. Once again I wanted to thank them. For being there. For being such great friends. For anything and everything that would allow me to keep talking and not move on. To not have to knock on the door. To not have to face her. To ask her. To hear her answer.

Instead, against every echo of *no* that rebounded in my head, I took a deep breath and walked on.

When I faced the cabin, my chest felt as though it might explode. Each step forward spread a wave of uncertainty and fear through my body. The sound of gravel beneath my feet could have been louder than anything in the world. Next to the chimes. They may as well have been alarms sounding my approach, a witch's best security from intruders.

189

I stopped at the porch, foot hovering over the horrible warped and greyish wooden planks. I wanted to run. To be anywhere but on her doorstep. Sweat bathed my palms, making the box more slippery than it already was.

It was time.

It had to work.

My foot landed. The boards welcomed me. I reached for the screen door. It parted with a grating creak.

For Mama.

For Mitch.

For me.

Please God.

Knuckles hit wood. The beat was hollow. Thunderous. Three knocks of terror splitting my soul. The box shook. No, my hands shook. Everything shook. My throat tightened.

Footsteps approached from within. Wood groaned. A lock turned, ripping through me like gunshot. The door parted. Slowly, an inch or more for a light-blue eye to peer upon me, then faster. Until the door met a wall. Until she stood before me. Watching me. Searching my thoughts with her magic. Unraveling the truths of who I was and what I wanted.

Short, a bit on the heavy side, she pulled a floral robe tight around her. Her eyes cut to Mo and Reggie, then back, deep lines on her round face adding to the dread building inside me.

I opened my mouth. I couldn't find words. We stood there for what felt like hours, staring at one another, waiting. Then I looked into her eyes and opened the box. Recognition flared. Her expression softened. I saw her kindness. I saw her pity.

I did everything I could to tell her why I was there. Everything I could to say that my brother was in the box. Everything I could to plead with her to bring him back. To give me my brother. To let him not be gone.

But it all fell in a wash of pain and sorrow and despair and my words failed and everything within me broke.

When I started crying, the *something* let loose.

It took me whole and left me certain I'd never feel anything good again.

24

My entire body shook. If I didn't move soon,
I was going to collapse in a quivering ball.
Into a puddle of tears and snot. After a low
nasal sigh, she closed the lid of the box, gently
placed her hand on my back and led me forward.
"Come on, son," the witch said, grated voice just
above a whisper. "In you go."

My head felt like a lead weight. I couldn't lift
my gaze. The world was a canvas of blue cardboard, encompassing all I could see. All I could
bear to see. Each step dragged, lifting only enough
to push to the next. Along the old wooden planks
of the patio. Through the doorway. Onto pine
flooring that creaked beneath my feet. An aroma
of incense filled the air. The room was brighter
than I'd expected. Cooler. I stopped on a woven
oval rug, rings of red, orange, yellow, and brown,
looking like a Thanksgiving Day archery bullseye.

Despite the continued tears, which had started a river of snot my sleeve couldn't keep up with,
I managed to take in the room through a sheet of
blurred wetness. I wiped at my eyes with the back

of my hand, one leg lifted to balance the box on my thigh. I could see for a few seconds, but the tears weren't stopping. My eyes burned like I'd rubbed pepper into them.

A small brown sectional sofa lay ahead, across from a stone fireplace blackened by years of use. A cushioned red rocker sat next to it, knitting needles buried in a ball of green yarn, a half-finished afghan draped over the wooden arm of the chair. A cup of tea rested on an end table between the chair and sofa, perspiration fogging the blue-tinted glass. From the corner of the room, a white rotating fan hummed, wobbly on its stand.

"Have a seat," said the witch, pointing my way to the sofa. She rounded me to take her place in the rocker.

I edged between a rectangular coffee table and the sofa and sat, box cradled, eyes on the day's paper on the polished wooden surface of the table. I didn't know what to say. I couldn't bring myself to look at her.

The rocker moaned as she collapsed into it. Her feet, covered in fuzzy black slippers, drew together, hands atop one another in her lap. She took a sip of tea, cleared her throat, then leaned back. When I looked up, I found her staring at me—into me—face hard and set, eyes cold and impatient. My cheeks quivered as I fought to stop the wave of tears.

I knew what I needed to say. I knew the offer. I knew she was going to wait me out because she couldn't perform the magic without hearing it from me first. But between the crying and the fear, I couldn't form the words. Lost for what to do, I pulled the card from beneath my shirt. Dale Murphy smiled back. Telling me it would all be fine. That he was ready to take his turn at the plate, and I should be too.

"You're Mark Murphy," she said, the sharpness of her tone and jagged edge of her drawl startling me enough to temporarily bring me back to the world. "And that, in the box, is your brother Mitch. I've been expecting you."

Unable to produce voice of any kind, I nodded. She waited. I swallowed hard and forced a response, which came in a rush like a waterfall. "How did you know?"

The smile she produced wasn't one of humor. It was pitying. For my ignorance, no doubt. Of course she'd know. Witches had to have ways of keeping up with the world. "Knowing what's plainly before you doesn't take skill. Or magic. It's accepting a truth that troubles us. That troubles you."

"Troubles me? What—"

"So, let's get on with it, or we'll be here all day. Tell me why you're here."

As if she had keyed an engine to life, my vision blurred again. I set the box down on the table and wiped the tears clear. For a lingering moment, I just stared at the shoebox, fighting a tightness building again in my chest. I fumbled with the lace around my neck, hands shaking like mad, clumsily removed it. I held the card out in quivering palms. Why was I so afraid? Why couldn't I just say it and let her do her work?

"Mitch … there was an accident. Car. He didn't … He …." The tears were back in full force, streaking my cheeks, dripping from my chin to my jeans. My breath came choppy, like my lungs had shrunk to half their size.

She rocked. Patient. Calm. No sign of emotion. No hint of feeling at all for what I was going through. There was only intense accusation and an unwillingness to budge. "You have to say it. We can't move forward until you accept it. Until you hear yourself admit the truth."

I shifted on the sofa, leaning closer to the box, then further away, then back. Finally, I lifted the lid, pulling the edge a bit too quickly, tearing the softened corner halfway across. Several seconds passed as I stared at the bag. At the ashes. At what remained of my brother. I set the card down beside it. Stared at her. Pleading.

I couldn't say it.

I didn't want to.

"You're afraid of making it real," she offered, again slicing into my thoughts as if they scrolled around the outside of my head like ticker tape.

"It doesn't have to be real," I said, with more strength than I'd expected. "It doesn't have to be. It can't be. I don't want it to be."

She took another drink of tea. Rocked in her chair. "The sun rises without your blessing. But you can't face the day until you wake. Sleeping through the light doesn't mean the day didn't happen."

I buried my confusion in a sleeve-swipe of my snotty nose. "What?"

She brought the rocker to a stop. It creaked heavy, long, like a wailing protest. Her hands came together over her chest and she glared at me, eyebrows raised. "Make it real, Mark."

There seemed to be no position I could sit in which everything didn't feel the most uncomfortable it had ever been. I began to wonder if it was the couch or her causing it. I looked away. At the pictures on the wall of a young boy. Around my age. Dark hair. A wide smile. Very pale. In some pictures he stood by a woman. Younger, but clearly the witch. I looked away, guilty for prying into her past; but the stuffed badger further along the wall on a shelf scared me enough to bring my attention back to the ashes. Back to Mitch. Back to the truth.

"I brought this." I lifted and dropped the card on the table. "It was mine. My cousin cheated me to get it. He thought ... He ... It meant a lot to him. That he took it from me. He was ... It was his car. He was the one who did this. It's his fault."

She didn't react. Didn't even look at the card. As if she'd turned into one of her stuffed animals, she just stared forward. At me. Prying into my thoughts.

I clawed at my hair. Wished I was a turtle so I could just pull my head into my shell and talk without seeing her eyes. So she couldn't see what I was thinking. "He was fine. It isn't fair. He's fine and my brother ... Mitch is ... It should have been Gordon."

She didn't waste a moment this time, kicking the wounded part of me like it was pure sport, her tone sharp. "The word, Mark. Say it."

It settled in my throat like acid. Burned. I tried to force it back, to wall off the pain it brought with it, but I knew I couldn't any longer. I knew she wouldn't help me without it.

"Dead," I said, generating a new wave of pain and tears. "Mitch is dead."

The word echoed around my head, rebounded, and chopped into my soul. Another onslaught of sobs followed, as bad or worse than the ones at the door. A day's worth spilled out at once. And memories of all the things lost along the way—reminders of the brother I loved so much—spiked each breath like a dagger to my chest.

She let me cry. Made no effort to console me. No move to give me comfort. I have no idea how long it lasted, but when I finally found my voice again, she was already up from her rocker, halfway across the room. "Please bring him back."

Nearly in the adjacent hall, she came to a stop. Gave me a quick look over her shoulder, then walked on, soles of her slippers scratching along the floor like sandpaper. Out of sight. A door groaned as it parted from its frame. Floorboards creaked. A drawer opened and shut. She returned and sat in the rocker, producing a small square photo from her palm. It dropped on the table beside the box.

"You asked how I knew who you were. That plus the story in the paper about the accident was all I needed."

It was a photo of me.

My school photo from this past year.

"How?" was all I could manage.

"Mitch gave it to me. When he visited with your rabbit. Zippy, was it?"

I nodded. Poked at the corner of the picture with a finger, then pushed it away. I remembered that day. Mitch and I went to the Mall after school to do some repairs. He brought his boombox and we listened to the radio. It was a good day. One of my favorites. But I didn't want to remember it. I didn't want to remember any of them anymore. "Why did he give you a picture of me?"

She held for a breath, leaned back full in the rocker. "Because it's the thing that meant the most to him. What he loved more than anything in the world was you."

Initially, the sentiment hit me like a boulder rolling downhill. Much though I thought the pain couldn't feel any worse, it managed to reach the core of my heart and tear it to shreds. But the thought that I was what he loved most, the realization of what that meant to the witch, the understanding of why he would give that to her when he brought Zippy, brought me to my feet in a flash, a sheet of ice cold draping me, saturating me, suffocating every last ounce of hope I carried with me.

"No! He didn't! That's not possible! He wouldn't do that!"

She eyed the photo. "And yet, he willingly offered it in exchange. For your rabbit. To ensure you didn't have to face the pain, the loss, the grief of losing it."

"No! He said he brought a toy from the neighbor's dog! It was supposed to be—"

"And I told him I'm no dog killer. Animal for an animal. Pure hooey."

I didn't know what to say, so I just shook my head. When that wasn't enough, I picked up the photo and threw it at her. Didn't do much good. The picture just fluttered to the ground at my feet. Undeterred, I shot up, voice rising like one of Mama's tidal waves of anger. "But I brought him here and this card! You can't … He wouldn't have done that! That wouldn't make any sense at all! Give himself up for Zippy? That's not a fair trade at all! Why would you let him do that?"

After a few rocks, she shrugged. "It isn't on me to decide what people should do with the life they're given. Any more than it's on you."

My heart sank. Sweat drained from my pores, cooling me to shivers. "You can still bring him back, though. Can't you? Just because he did that doesn't mean anything, right?"

The witch stilled in her chair. Gripped the arms and pushed herself upright. "You're not going to understand this for a while, Mark, but there are consequences to our choices. What your brother did—bringing that rabbit to me—he did for you. He never questioned it. Never blinked when he gave me that picture. That's how much he loved you. How important you were to him.

He was willing to put his life on the line for your happiness."

Some part of my brain thought maybe she was trying to help, but every word felt like a needle jabbing my heart, picking at whatever was left of the dam holding my pain in place. Tired of the crying, tired of the snot, tired of her nonsense, I found a nice home in my anger. "Is that why he died?" I almost choked on the word. But the anger soothed me. "This is your fault! You should have never accepted his offer! What good is it to bring back a rabbit but lose my brother? That's stupider than an animal for an animal! Why didn't you tell him no? Why didn't you send him away and tell him to forget you existed? That his brother need-ed him way more than any rabbit! *You* did this! I hate you!"

"I thought your cousin was to blame?" She stood and shuffled by me, toward the kitchen. "You'll need to make up your mind about that."

The fury consumed me. I wanted to throw things at her. She didn't even seem to care that Mitch was gone. That my brother was dead be-cause of her. "You have to fix this! I did ... I *stole* him from my mother to bring him here! I have the card! I have ... I have...." My pack. Reggie and Mo had my pack. "I have Gordon's gun! I can go get it!"

That brought her smarmy haughtiness to a stop real quick. But I didn't much care for the look that followed it. Made Mama's mad face look like a clown at a carnival. "I'm going to overlook the fact that a boy your age is walking around with a gun and assume you weren't suggesting you'd use it on me."

"No!" The shock of such a thing knocked my anger down a few pegs. "No, I just meant it was Gordon's. It meant everything to him. That and the card. That should be enough, right? It doesn't matter what Mitch did. It doesn't matter. You made a mistake. You have to bring him back, right?"

She tugged at the ties of her robe. Let free a deep sigh. "I tell you what I *have* to do. I *have* to make you some hot cocoa while you clean your face up. You look like a pig after eating out a trough of slime. Use the bathroom down the hall and clean up. Don't want you blubbering in a mug of perfectly good cocoa. I imagine, if you'll take your time with it, let the sun hit you through the window, you'll feel different when you return. Cocoa will be waiting."

"Hot cocoa?" I watched her into the kitchen. A towel hung from the fridge door. It had roses and other flowers on it. It opened just enough for her to pull out some milk. "What kind of witch are you?"

She opened a nearby cupboard and grabbed a white ceramic mug. "The kind that makes hot cocoa for crying boys, apparently. Now, go clean up."

Much though I wanted to refuse, to stand there until she acknowledged none of this would have happened if she had just sent Mitch away to begin with, I didn't have much dry sleeve left and needed to blow my nose. If I could do that on one of her towels, all the better.

I was up and out of sight in the best thunderous stomp I could manage.

The hall was narrow and dark. More pictures hung on the wall, various frames of the young boy from before, capturing smiling shots all the way back to his days of crawling. Near the end of the hall, I found the bathroom. The light above the mirror cast a yellowish hue, which did nothing to make me feel better about my snotty and swollen face. My eyes were bloodshot. Cheeks a splotchy bright red I'd only ever seen on apples.

I passed up a hand towel—Mama would have killed me if she knew I even considered it—and grabbed a wad of toilet paper. There seemed to be no end to the mess in my nose. Took several blows to feel the slightest bit of relief. Even then it kept coming. Trying my best to avoid the mirror, I splashed warm water in my face, rubbed it in my eyes, even wet my hair a little to keep it from falling over my forehead. The ceramic sink felt cool against my palms. I shut the water off and leaned over the edge of the basin, mind whirring, the tears waiting their turn.

She'll bring him back.

She has to.

But Mitch is dead.

He's dead.

A loud *thump* shot me out of my thoughts, nearly scared me enough to scream. It came from outside the window. Carefully, expecting some demon or evil pet befitting a witch, I pulled back the white frilly curtains and peered through the muddy glass. It took a moment to take in what I saw. Then my brain threw out an idea I didn't care for at all. One I didn't want to be real. Especially considering what it would mean.

Wrapping around the back of the cottage, several wide pens held maybe a dozen goats, some sleeping, some quietly munching on hay. A doghouse and pen lay beside the goats, offering the faintest shadow of a large bloodhound, on its side and kicking its way through a dream. The posts of another pen hovered just in sight. Whatever animal was penned in wasn't making itself known.

But it was the large woodshed straight ahead that drew my full attention. It rested on a bed of gravel, slanted tin roof held aloft by the same kind of four-by-four posts we'd used to corner the Mall. The front sat open to the world, each side covered by slatted two-by-fours. The entire structure looked solid, but it had clearly seen quite a few seasons. The wood was bleached by the sun, a little warped in spots from the humidity. On the gravel floor, the witch had built in tables, affixed to each wall, all the way around the interior.

On each table lay a rectangular cage. Six in all.

In each cage, a rabbit hopped, ate, jumped, or slept. Five of them were anything from brown and white to reddish-brown. One of them was an albino.

Another *thump* issued as the rabbit in the center kicked. Hay shot out to the cage's edge.

My heart pounded. For a moment, a wave of dizziness passed me by as I watched the rabbits frolic. The pain returned. My chest hurt. My throat tightened. Tears welled. I waited. And waited. And waited.

Then my entire body went warm. Still. My vision cleared. I could breathe.

And I knew my brother was dead.

25

The rocker creaked as she teetered back and forth, knitting furiously in a way that still seemed calm and easy. On the table, a mug of hot cocoa steamed beside the box, the baseball card almost touching the base of the white ceramic. Much though I wanted to ease to the sofa, the boards wouldn't let me, each step broadcasting louder than a cannon. Despite the noise, the witch didn't look up.

No. Not *witch*.

She didn't look up.

"Did he know?" My voice sounded distant, as if someone else had spoken. A tremble struck me, from my shoulders down to my feet. I fought against more tears. That moment of acceptance was sliding away fast. I didn't much care for the reality it brought behind it.

"Know what?"

I stopped a few feet shy of the sofa, unwilling to look at the box. Somehow it seemed wrong to have my eyes on my brother's ashes when asking a question with an answer I knew I didn't want.

"That it wasn't Zippy."

The knitting needles stopped. She set them aside, carefully looping the free strands around the skein of yarn. When she looked up, it wasn't the same face. She might have been a different woman altogether. There were lines in her face, wrinkles in her forehead. Her skin looked weathered. A gentleness teased at the corner of her mouth. She looked tired.

"People tend to believe what they want to believe," she said, almost apologetic. "A lot easier than having to believe something they don't want. For what it's worth, I'd say your brother believed what he *needed* to believe so he could lift your spirits. That's why he was willing to lay himself down for you. Probably thought he'd outsmarted me. That I wouldn't call his bluff. He put his love for you out front and figured that would be enough to get what he wanted. Damn smart boy. Saw my friends out the window, did you?"

"Yeah."

She nodded. "Hoped you would. You seem like a bright boy. Like your brother. How's Leonard doing?"

"Leonard?" She looked at me, eyebrows raised. "Oh. The rabbit. He's well. Got a cage he stays in," I lied. I didn't want to tell her he'd gone and run off to who knew where.

She seemed good with that answer and went back to knitting.

For a while longer, I stood in place, heaving deep breaths to stem the press of sadness. I don't know if she was always so patient with folks, or if it was just for me, but she seemed content to wait me out.

"What's your name?"

Her head turned in a snap, like a curious dog presented a treat. A smile spread, short lived but potent. Full of warmth. "You know? Nobody's ever asked."

To that, I could only shrug. My gaze set somewhere on the wall over her shoulder, I edged to the sofa and sat. Finally, drawn to it like a bee to a flower, I eyed the box. "Mitch said that names honor the person. They give us an identity. Give us a place in the world. He said I should always ask. Out of respect. And kindness."

"Mitch was a good boy," she said, after clearing her throat, settling in the chair as if she'd suddenly been prodded. "I could see that in the short time he was here. First person to ever come up here looking to cure someone else's grief rather than their own. That mattered to me. Told me all I needed to know about him. Name's Louise Grimes."

I nodded. Looped my finger around the lace holding the card. "You're not a witch."

A laugh like a cough found freedom. She rocked a few times. "I'm what people want to believe I am. Whatever they need to cope. Granted, I don't get the visitors I used to, so there isn't much talk about what I am now. Just stories. From grown-ups who were once kids. Kids who lost pets. Lost loved ones. Most of them never came up here. Those who did, though, well, I may have played my part. To a point. I just wanted to be left alone, honestly. Left to my own grief."

I eyed the pictures on the wall. Found her following my lead when I looked back.

"My son," she offered, a slight wince pinching her eyes to slits. "Davey. He was a good boy, too. A lot like you and Mitch. A few months after his fourteenth birthday, he was diagnosed with leukemia. Wasn't long after that. I just … I didn't cope well. Left my practice—I was a grief counselor if you'll believe that. Guess I never shook the work off. My husband handled it all worse than I did. He left and never looked back. So, I came up here. Away from it all. I quit," she said near a whisper, the regret in her expression fading as she faced me. Forced a smile for my benefit.

"The taxidermy was a way to process it all. Friend of mine taught me how years before Davey died. It was something to keep my mind busy. Give some semblance of life to things that had lost it. But it only got people talking. And eventually, they started looking. Standing out on the road like I couldn't see them whispering and pointing. So, I tried harder to keep them away. I guess screaming like a banshee in my night gown at kids didn't do anything to discourage the witch talk." She shrugged.

The squeak of her rocker filled the silence. I pulled the lace back around my neck. Tucked the card in my shirt. I wouldn't need it. Mitch was dead. He wasn't coming back. Again, I had to take a deep breath. The sadness was threatening to take over.

"He isn't really gone," she said, still managing to read my thoughts even without the inner sight of a witch.

The tears were back. Quick, light, but lining up one after the next. I wiped them away. "You mean he's in Heaven? Mama told me that. Doesn't really help."

"Heaven, Hell, Paradise, Purgatory, whatever suits you. All just places the dead have to deal with. It's those still alive that are left to deal with the loss. The void. Feeling like a part of ourselves has been ripped away and we'll never be whole again."

I nodded, knocking free more tears that streaked my cheeks and fell to my legs.

"People are going to tell you that it'll get better, and to some extent they're right. Time stretches feelings thinner than we realize. Little consolation, but true. They'll say life will return to normal someday, that you'll find a way to move forward again, just like you used to; but that's as true as telling someone what God thinks. Losing someone takes them out of your life. Takes that part of your life—that day-to-day part they shared with you—with it. Whatever you are without them physically in your world, that's the new normal. Like losing a leg. Life won't be the same ever again. But you'll walk, if you want. You'll find a new normal if you have the strength. Mitch is gone, and now you have to deal with that. You have to let yourself feel it. Don't run from it. Be sad. Share that pain and loss with others who also feel it. With those who share love with you. But never think he's gone from who you are, Mark. Never you think it."

Whatever resolve I had left I relinquished. I tried to nod. Tried to let her know I heard her words, tried to fight the tidal wave of pain, but it didn't help. I buried my face in my hands and cried. At some point, she sat next to me, cradled me in her arm and held me tight.

26

I don't know how long I was there. A clock on the kitchen wall said it was a touch after four in the afternoon when she walked me to the door, but I hadn't checked it when I arrived. It felt like hours had passed. Days. Only as the door parted and the brightness of outdoor light faded did I remember Reggie and Mo were waiting. They sprang up from the ground in unison, halfway down the driveway, hands dug in pockets, eyes wide.

Relief and hesitation washed over me. I was happy beyond measure to see them. Happy to have friends so determined to help that they'd undertake this kind of trip for me. Even knowing the result before I did. I was happier to return to them than I'd ever been. But equally, I didn't want to face them. Didn't want to tell them what they already knew. Didn't want to walk back to them with the box in hand and explain with real words that my brother was gone, and nothing would bring him back.

The thought alone choked me up. I'd had several moments in the cottage when the pain would release, the tears would stop, and I'd feel like the worst had passed. Then I'd picture Mitch, smiling at me as he taught me how to hit, as we worked on the Mall, as we sat in our room talking about music or baseball or movies or anything at all. And the tears would start all over.

I couldn't believe he'd never be there again. That I'd be in that room alone going forward.

Ms. Grimes didn't say much else. She just let me cry. Forced the hot cocoa into my hands and encouraged me to drink. She was probably a great mother to Davey. Eventually, she suggested I be on my way, back home, before it got too much later.

I hugged the box tight, a bottle of soda in each hand. For Reggie and Mo. They were probably pretty thirsty. I couldn't even remember her giving them to me.

Two steps from the door, I paused. Turned back to see her nodding encouragingly. "Go on, now. Get yourself, and your friends, home safely."

The stuffed animals strewn about were less scary than they had been before. The air felt cooler. The sky brighter. "Do you know Officer John?"

Ms. Grimes frowned, chin raised as if she were searching the name in her brain. "John Hartley? Boling County sheriff?"

I nodded. "He said what you did was a sin. I don't like that people think of you like that."

For a moment, I thought she might take offense, but then she laughed. Lost in memory. "My word, did he? That sounds a bit harsh, don't you think? Especially given he came up here himself. A long time ago."

"He came up here? Why?"

"Lost his dog and wanted what everyone wants. To hope. To believe in magic. To have what isn't there anymore returned to them. He was one of the first ones I shooed off. Certainly not one of the last who took their frustrations out on my image. I mostly stopped dealing with folks after that. Let the stories be what they were. Honestly, until Mitch, I hadn't much more than opened the door for anyone in years. But he had kindness. Heart. I could see it. Same as when you stood in the same spot. With the same kind of box."

The thought warmed me a bit. My mind wandered to an image of a young Officer John and his dog, standing where I stood. To the countless others. "Why did you do it? Why even talk to people when you knew there was nothing you could do?"

Ms. Grimes straightened, eyes flashing wide briefly. "Well, now. That's a Big Question, isn't it? Why does anyone do anything, really? I suspect if we knew that answer, we likely wouldn't do the things we needed to do to grow and learn and be more. Why did you come up here?" she asked, a thin smile guiding her. "Maybe because it was all you *could* do. The only way you could move forward. Maybe don't think about 'why.' Think about what's gained from it."

I gave it a moment's thought. Nodded. "I can live with that."

The clap of the door sounded as I walked off. Gravel crunched beneath my feet. The scent of pine filled the air. Reggie and Mo shifted uncomfortably until I reached them. I handed the sodas over, which neither opened. They just held the bottles, staring at me. Reggie flinched, like she wanted to hug me. I must have looked horrible. Enough that even Mo could tell through his blurred vision.

It stirred the pain, which bubbled and boiled until I thought it might spill out. I picked up my pack and tucked the box away, zipped it as far as it would go without much care for perfection. "Can we go home now?" I asked, walking on before they could respond.

With every part of my being, I wanted to tell them everything. They deserved it. They'd certainly earned at least that. But each time I opened my mouth, my throat tightened, and the tears welled. We were halfway down Spook Hill Road before Reggie said anything.

"Are you okay?"

The tears came. As much for Mitch as for what I felt for my friends. "No. My brother's dead."

Her hand looped in mine. She squeezed hard. Mo's arm draped over my shoulder. I thought I might start sobbing again, but it didn't come. The hurt was the same. The pain as intense as ever, but it was like I didn't have the strength for it. Didn't have any tears left to shed.

Or maybe my friends just made it easier.

We walked in silence to Highway 100. After a couple of cars whizzed by, tires on wet pavement sounding a lot like speeding zippers, we crossed the road and walked along the shoulder toward the overpass. Spots of blue showed through the blanket of thinning grey clouds. The sun trying to return. To make the skies feel normal again.

On the overpass, we paused to look down on the creek. Mo and Reggie drained their drinks. Closer to Spook Hill, the water rushed faster, piles of debris thicker on the banks. It was loud enough that Mo had to raise his voice for us to hear him.

"I'd like to stick to kiddie pools in the future, if you don't mind."

It made me laugh. Like a hiccup of noise, but nice all the same.

We walked on. Stopped again at the edge of the road. The woods loomed beyond. Thick and unforgiving.

"What about the bear?" asked Reggie.

"Damn. Forgot." I wiped at my face.

"We can't stay here," said Mo. "My mother's going to tear me to shreds when I get home as it is. I'd rather not add 'eaten by a bear' to my sins."

A car passed in a great hurry, the wind pressing us forward a step as it sped on along the two-lane road. Red lights flared on the back of the car as the driver landed hard on the brakes, slowing it considerably as it passed the outline of a white car heading our way about a half-mile down.

"Let's just go," I said, already making my way down the embankment toward the woods. "Just stay as quiet as possible. We'll keep close to the creek and watch for any sign of tracks. Move fast and maybe we can get through quick. I guess, worst case, we're all going for a ride in the creek again."

As close to jogging as we could get, we hit the woods and cut toward the creek. The ground was wet, but not as bad as it had been. At any sign of overgrowth, we wove around until it cleared. After about five minutes, the trees and briars forced us further into the woods. Weaving and bobbing around trees, we made good time.

Briars forced me to the right of a wide-trunked oak. I was even with it when a branch about the size of a lead pipe swung into view. It caught me solid in the chest, knocking the air from my lungs, sending the world into a hazy shade of black. I tumbled, struggling to catch my breath, pain throbbing through my ribs.

Something heavy pressed into my neck, forced my face into the ground as my pack was wrestled free of one arm, then the other. Garbled shouts and screams filtered through the hammer of my pulse, the ringing in my ears. The smell of wet soil filled my nostrils. The weight lifted and I pushed off the ground, rolled to see Mo and Reggie leap onto someone, tangles of arms and legs flailing about, my pack at the center.

27

Even in that flash of a second, with my friends struggling to free my pack, and my chest feeling like it had been split open, I still wondered how it was that I hadn't expected it. Hadn't given any thought to the fact that Gordon wouldn't give up. That he never gave up. Once he decided he was doing something, that was it. Come hell or high water. Usually both.

Mitch's map on the ground gave answer to any question as to how he found us.

My fault. Again.

Blood had soaked through the entire left leg of his jeans. His sneaker was dark red. The pale of his face was ghostly, skin coated in glossy sweat. Every step, every movement seemed a struggle he wouldn't best. He looped his right arm through the straps of the pack and pulled it free, left arm all but dangling at his side. Reggie and Mo threw their empty pop bottles at him but missed badly. Then they tackled him. When his shoulder crashed into the ground, he let out a scream.

Fueled by the pain in his cracked shoulder blade, Gordon swung his right arm outward, clocking Mo in the jaw with a closed fist. Mo crumpled to the ground like an android getting its power shut off, out cold.

Reggie held on as Gordon rose unbalanced to his feet, her hands tight on a slight opening in the top pouch of the pack. The zipper pulled back with each tug, revealing more of the blue corner of the shoebox. Against a wave of dizziness, I managed to get upright and charge. But before I could get to them, Gordon kicked out, his bloody shoe squaring up with Reggie's leg. With a yelp of pain, she dropped, clutching her knee.

Gordon made to run but staggered into a tree, hand clawing at the bark to find a grip. To stay on his feet. It gave me enough time to hook one of the straps, quickly looping it to my elbow. He was way stronger, no matter how injured and beat he was. With each tug of the other strap, my feet slid. Something tore at the base of a strap, more stitches popping loose the longer we pulled.

"Give ... me ... my ... pack!"

His eyes tightened, teeth bared, feet set as if he were about to pull as hard as he could. Then, without warning, and with a shout from the pain issuing from his shoulder, his left hand dropped into the unzipped opening, seized the box, and he let go of the pack. With all my weight shifted to counter his, I hit the ground hard, inciting another burst of fire in my chest.

Gordon smiled wide against a broken, almost crazed, laugh, backed to run, but failed to notice Reggie's leg stretched out behind him. With his one good leg taken out, he fell backward, cradling the box as he landed solid on his rear.

"God dammit!" he shouted. "What the hell is it with you all anyway?"

I'd like to say I thought my actions through. That I considered what I was doing. But it'd be a lie. All I knew was that there was no way Gordon was leaving with Mitch's ashes. Fury stole over me. Everything burned, all pain taken away, all thought of anything but giving Gordon what he deserved snuffed out like a candle's flame.

Like a gunslinger drawing his weapon from a holster, I withdrew the gun from my pack and pointed it at Gordon. I'd never shot a gun, never even touched one until the Junkyard, but I was sure I knew how to pull a trigger. Knew how much damage a bullet could cause.

I stood, shaky gun aimed at him, every inch of his face flashing from anger to shock to anger again.

"Is that my gun?" he asked, accusatory no matter the sight of it pointed at his chest.

I backed a few steps as he stood.

"Yeah," I said, strong enough to sound calm, despite how insanely scared I felt doing what I had done.

"The hell you have my gun for, you dumbass little shit? Did you take that from the car too?"

I nodded. "Give me the box. Now."

"Mark," said Reggie, hands tight around her knee. She shook her head when I glanced down at her. "Don't. It's not who you are."

"I have to. It's his fault." Then to Gordon, as much anger rising as I'd ever felt, "You have to pay for what you did! Give him back to me, now!"

He managed a laugh, which firmed my grip on the gun. No way he was laughing about this. No way.

"Give him back? Give who—" Confusion came and went. The pale tone of his face fell even whiter, almost see through. Slowly, as if expecting a snake to strike, he eased the corner of the shoe-box lid. For a few seconds he stared within. Then he tipped the lid back and nearly choked.

It looked like he'd turned to stone. Like it had been Medusa's head in there, not Mitch's ashes. A squeak of voice emerged from the back of his throat as he dropped the box. It hit the ground with a thud, lid bouncing, the dusty remains in the baggie shifting.

Gordon lifted his gaze to me, bottom lip trembling. "What the hell is that?"

"What do you think it is, you baboon?" snapped Reggie. "It's his brother's ashes. The one you killed with your car!"

"That's—" He swallowed hard, eyes wide. "That's Mitch." It wasn't a question. He almost whispered it.

Over the barrel of the shaking gun, I stared at him. Felt my anger fade as his eyes brimmed with tears that wouldn't fall, as he dropped to his knees a foot from the open box. It hit me, as hard as the branch to my chest.

"You didn't know I had that." Gordon didn't look up. Just shook his head. "You didn't even know about the gun. You thought I had something else."

His breath heaved, then fell in a choppy blast. Hesitantly, he reached out, two fingers touching the bag until it gave enough for him to feel the contents. He stroked the medallion a few times then recoiled at the soot on his fingertips. "Stash. In the passenger's seat. I kept it there. Taped over."

I could see the seat as clear as I had earlier. Torn. No, cut. Stuffing puffed out as if it had been dug through. "It wasn't there. Someone had already gotten to it. You thought I had it. That's why you were chasing us."

"Thought you were going to the cops," he mumbled, voice distant, as if it had come from elsewhere.

"Could have just given it to Officer John at the Junkyard if I was."

To my surprise, he laughed. Shook his head. "Yeah. Guess so. Didn't think. Just got angry. Like always." After a few seconds, he looked up, blinked as if he'd forgotten about the gun. "Where were you taking him?"

I thought about leaving it be. Keeping that between me and my friends. But the gun was still there. Still aimed at him. I wanted him to know. Wanted him to understand I was serious. Not that he needed the entire truth. "The witch on Spook Hill. I wanted her to bring him back. To take you instead. But he'd already made a deal with her when he took Zippy up there."

"Witch?" Gordon looked around, as if only then realizing he was in the woods. "Spook Hill? The bitty whose house we cased two years ago?"

"Cased? You mean you and Mitch have been there before?"

For a few seconds, he held quiet. Staring at the ashes. "We'd heard the stories, so we went looking. Just curious. Weren't gonna do nothing to her. It was night. We snuck around. She had a bunch of animals. Goats and rabbits and shit. Dog barked and she came out of the house in her nightgown screaming like a nut case. We took off."

"Mitch saw the rabbits? That's how he knew about Zippy. He knew."

"Who's Zippy?"

"He didn't tell you he went back up there." I shouldn't have been surprised by that. Why would he? Gordon wouldn't have understood. He would have laughed at us both for believing in it.

"Tell me what?"

"Never mind. Doesn't matter. Point is, I wanted you to pay for killing my brother. Still do."

Mo stirred. Moved, but didn't wake. Blood trickled from a gash on his forehead.

"You keep saying that."

"I keep meaning it. You should pay for killing him."

The laugh returned. Like a snort of air. "No, you keep saying 'my brother.' Like he wasn't mine too."

"He wasn't."

"Nah. Not as such. But family by blood all the same. Best family I knew. Like a brother to me in every way. Spent every day since I was five with him. Every day. He was the only one who had my back. Only one who gave a rat's ass about me. Only one …" He trailed off, gaze locked again on the ashes. "Now he's gone. Just like that. Gone."

Save for the crunch of an unseen animal or some such on leaves and limb in the distance, the woods went silent. Gordon blinked several times, his lips moving but no words coming out. Like he was in prayer, only saying the same thing over and over. Finally, a whisper of voice emerged, his mouth working faster, the words "my fault" rising faster and louder.

Then he snapped to, stopped, watery eyes meeting mine.

"Do it."

"Do what?"

"Shoot me. Do it. I killed him. He told me not to do lines before we left the party. He told me. I did it anyway. About fought him rather than give him the keys. I don't remember nothing after I started the engine. So, do it, Murph. Get your vengeance. I got nothing to live for anyway. Not with what I've done. Thought I could push it off. Thought it'd all sort itself out. But it won't. I did this. So do it. Cops were already after me anyway.

If they found my stash, then they know what I've done. They'll add killing Mitch to it."

He closed his eyes and waited, mouthing "Do it, do it, do it."

A vision of Mitch woke me up. If he'd been there, he'd have torn into me for thinking about shooting Gordon. No matter what he'd done. He was a great brother. To us both. I looked down at the gun in horror and dropped it like it was hot, one hand pinning the other to my chest.

Before Gordon opened his eyes, I knelt to the ground and grabbed the lid of the box. Dragged it away from him. When his eyes did open, they fell on the spot. Drifted over towards the gun. He reached out for it, fingers wrapping it, cradling it in his palm like he'd been reunited with a lost loved one.

Or a lost friend.

In a flash he was on his feet, gun out before him, aimed somewhere in my direction.

Then the woods erupted in foot fall, in voice, in chaos.

"Drop it!" Officer John charged from between a cluster of pines, out of breath, gun drawn on Gordon. "Get down, Mark!"

I didn't move.

But Gordon did.

With no hesitation, no further thought, he lifted the gun to his temple and pulled the trigger.

28

I couldn't bring myself to say anything the whole ride home. I sat in the back seat of Officer John's squad car, separated from him by a black metal grate. Mo and Reggie sat beside me, all of us staring out windows like there was nowhere else to look.

The shoebox rested in my lap. I kept it shut tight, one hand underneath, holding the wet bottom in place. After everything, it was amazing it hadn't disintegrated altogether. At least the bag hadn't busted. I'm not sure how I would have explained that to Mama.

Officer John had seen us run into the woods and chased after. It had been his car coming our way down 100. Part of me wished he hadn't. Not that things would have gone any different.

We were rounding the courthouse downtown, off toward the other end of Moody and eventually my home, when I finally looked back. The other squad car that Officer John called in—it had been the officer waving at folks from the tracks earlier—peeled off south on Silver Lake. The county precinct and jailhouse were about a mile that way.

Where Gordon would be put away. For who knew how long.

Justice, after all.

Would have been the way Mitch wanted it to end.

Officer John said the creek was to blame. Something about the water keeping the gun from firing. For reasons I couldn't even begin to put into words, I was glad. Not just because I didn't want to watch my cousin blow his brains out, but because, to my surprise, a part of me didn't want him to die at all. Ms. Grimes would say it was the part of me that Mitch lived in now. The part where he and I would still be together. Where he'd talk me through life with all his lessons, same as always. Mitch wouldn't have wanted Gordon to die. He tried, as it was when he was alive, to keep him away from trouble.

Mitch loved Gordon. I didn't need to understand why.

The car bounced as we pulled into the long drive. It was only then that I realized Mo and Reggie were looking at me. I didn't want to talk about it. Not then. When the car stopped and Officer John opened the door, I just said, "See ya," and got out.

Mama mobbed me, arms as tight around me as I'd ever felt. She was crying, but not the same kind of crying she'd done over Mitch. This was deeper. This was for me. Pretty quick, I joined her. She carted me inside without a word. Officer John drove Mo and Reggie home.

29

The ashes glowed red-hot, the torn sheet of poster rippling as the heat built underneath. The flame showed no mercy, igniting Susanna Hoffs' face first, then expanding outward. The paper blackened, curled as the fire moved away, then bits broke free and drifted into the air, rising higher and higher, vanishing in the shelter of leafy treetops.

"Damn shame," muttered Dunk, following the path of another piece of broken ash with a finger until it moved beyond his reach. "A hottie like that should start fires, not be burned by them."

"You're a real peach, Dunk. You'll make a great ex to a lot of women." Reggie tried to hold her expression, but it broke in a wide smile. Her laugh came as a high-pitched giggle. I'd never heard that before. Sometimes it seemed she was reclaiming a lot more of her girlhood with each year I knew her.

Which wasn't a bad thing.

Dunk hoisted his broken foot, finger-tapped the cast running up past his ankle. "Betty June signed my cast 'with love.' Sandra Hope signed it 'hope you can still dance.' Lisa Withers signed it with a heart. I think the ladies on my street appreciate me just fine."

"Or they pity you like a wet homeless dog," said Mo, his formidable head waggle and brow raise adding to the insult. He pressed his new glasses high on his nose.

"Hey, whatever it takes to get them to pet my—"

"Nope. Nope. You're not finishing that." Reggie stabbed a marshmallow on the end of a stick, head shaking enough to fling her silky black hair back and forth over her shoulders. She handed him the stick and began work on another.

The poster done and gone, the fire started to fade. I dug another piece of two-by-four from the pile of debris that was once the Mall. We'd broken or hacked most of them into smaller pieces the weekend before. Without any rain over the two weeks since it had fallen, the wood was dry and burned up quick.

Within a few seconds, flame licked up around the edge of the wood, crackled, and lit it. Three marshmallows hovered above, browning as they were turned. Dunk let his catch fire and waited until the charred remains almost dripped from his stick. Then, somehow, without even flinching, he buried the hot treat into his mouth.

While my friends laughed over the sticky mess they were making all over their faces, I slid my pack closer to my leg. The blue shoebox stuck

out, looking worn and near falling apart. I pulled
it free carefully, though I couldn't imagine why it
mattered anymore. A small sandwich-sized baggie lay within, half-full of some of Mitch's ashes.
We'd let the first half free at the ballfield. Had a
memorial for him there. I cried more than I was
comfortable with in the company of my friends,
but it somehow felt all right. Mo, Reggie and
Dunk crowded me in a group hug that brought
my tears to a stop.

"I still can't believe she gave some of them to
you," said Dunk.

I shrugged. Mama had been different since Officer John brought me home. She still cried, a lot,
but she wasn't drinking. She just wanted to spend
time with me. Talk about Mitch. Hold me. "She
thought Mitch would like being at the ballfield
and here. He spent enough time at both."

"What's she going to do with the rest?"

Again, I shrugged. Felt like I started most everything that way now. My daily life was nothing
more than one big shrug. "Keeping them for now.
Said when the right thing to do came along, she'd
know."

The baggie felt light in comparison to the larg-
er bag I'd carried before.

Or maybe it was the weight on my shoulders
that felt lighter.

I tossed the shoebox square on the plank of
wood charring from flame. It caught almost immediately. In a matter of seconds, it was gone.
Unlike the poster, it folded in on itself and tum-

bled into the firepit, where it became part of the ashes fueling the fire.

We watched it in silence.

I gave them all a quick smile, stood, and walked to where the Mall used to stand. They followed, gathered around me.

Dunk's father had dragged off the indoor carpet and helped tear the framing of the structure down. Officer John was kind enough to pitch in as well. He carted away anything with nails, took the bigger posts and pieces of wood, and left us enough kindling for this weekend. For the memorial.

He'd been around a lot more. Spending time with Mama and me. Can't say I didn't like it. We'd watched several Braves games together on TBS. He knew a ton about baseball. Said he'd work with me on my hitting. Even bought me a bat. One lighter, one I could manage.

The ground was all dirt, any grass or growth stamped out by the Mall living atop it for more than a year. I thought of Mitch, of the work we put in to build it. Of the laughs, the music from his boombox playing while we hammered away. Of the fact I never got the opportunity to camp here with him. Just the two of us.

Just you and me, right?

That was the one.

Tears welled.

It was time.

The baggie opened easily. I tipped it, moved it side to side as the ashes spilled out. At the ballfield, they'd gone into the grass. All but vanished from sight. Here, they sat atop the ground, bits of grey and white easy to make out. I gave thought to covering them, to spreading them around some more, but decided against it. I wasn't coming back out anyway. There was no need.

We'd talked about a rebuild. Maybe we would. But it wouldn't be here.

Reggie draped an arm around my shoulder, rested her head against my arm. She'd never acted that way before the trip to Spook Hill. In truth, I wouldn't have wanted her to. But two weeks of holding hands, walking together through the woods without Dunk or Mo around, and phone calls that were longer into the night than her daddy cared for, more than changed my mind about things. We hadn't kissed yet. It still felt weird to think that way. But I wasn't going to turn away when the chance came.

"You all right?" she asked.

"Yeah," I said, feeling it to my core. "I miss him. But he isn't gone. Not really. Not as long as I remember. Sounds strange, I know, but sometimes it feels like he's still here. Talking in my head. I guess that's something."

Wind rustled the pines, cutting through needles and leaves and rocking the trunks, which creaked like a bunch of frogs croaking at night.

"Life," said Mo, breathy voice guiding his arms outward, "is a mystery."

"Oh, Lord," groaned Dunk. "Should have known it would come to this."

Reggie laughed.

I thought about stopping him, thought I couldn't get there just yet, but his smile widened, and when I said nothing, he stepped back, voice rising.

"Everyone must stand alone." Again he held, but not for us. This was pure dramatics. Pure Mo. "I hear you call my name. And it feels like … home."

There was a moment, a few breaths, while he stood in place, arms closed over his chest, head bent low enough to drop his glasses to the tip of his nose. Then he looked up, beamed, and broke into dance.

"So, we're doing this?"

I gave Dunk a pat on the shoulder. "We're doing this."

"I gotta admit," Reggie said, as we watched Mo dance toward, then around, the fire, "he can dance. I'm kind of jealous."

Dunk popped another marshmallow into his mouth. I have no idea where he'd kept it until then. Mouth full, he said, "For a goober, yeah."

Mo started clapping in rhythm with music we couldn't hear. Then his vocals began, and he wound through the lyrics like only Mo could. Clear and beautiful, moves of his body solid and a little more *adult* than his mama would have liked.

Now in complete concert mode, Mo moved straight into performing. Leg kicks, finger waggles, tossing hair that wasn't there, he showed no sign of humility. He was built for the stage.

Dunk leaned forward, taking us both in. "Does anyone else feel weird about this? I'm not even sure he knows we're here anymore."

Despite all the dancing, his vocals never wavered. I had no idea what life had in store for Mo, but I had no doubt it involved being something people would remember. He hit the back end of a verse, waving wildly in our direction as he sang, "Let the choir sing!"

We didn't need the encouragement. We'd seen the show before and we knew our part. One by one, we joined him around the fire, singing the chorus loudly, clapping in beat, acting like complete and utter idiots with nothing better to do than be happy together.

Like friends.

Like family.

ACKNOWLEDGMENTS

This book is easily the most difficult work I've ever written. When I set out to write it, the emotional battle Mark endures was challenging enough, but along the way I lost an important member of my life and it brought the entire story to a screeching halt for two months. When I returned, I found myself unable to avoid channeling all my grief into Mark's journey. On one hand, that makes for some excellent reading. On the other, it still triggers that sense of loss every time I read it through. So, Maggie, your parting gift to me was one of unexpected greatness. For that, this book will always be the most special to me.

I would not be the writer I am without the constant critique, writing advice, and overall friendship of David L. Robbins. Without his guidance, I'd still be chopping away, believing I was good enough already, and would not have learned what it means to look past the hurt and hear the words. You're an unrelenting beast on the page, in life, and, of course, in fantasy baseball.

To the entire Broadleaf Writers Association team: Over the years the names and faces have changed, but each of you took hold of my dream and have made it into what it is today. You have helped build a writing community, fueled its engine with your passion for writing, and helped to create an organization that will not only advance the learning and connection to the craft of writing, but will help many writers realize their dream of publication. I thank you, love you, and wish all the best to each of you on your journey.

Of the many writing friends I've made over the years, I can think of no other as unique and important to my journey than John Adcox. Talking baseball was always the excuse for a conversation, but our talks on craft, on the business, and the many breakdowns of this manuscript and others helped focus my attention on the importance of proper storytelling. There is an order to all things, and for all things must there be order. Or something like that. It sounded profound, right? Anyway, thank you for putting me on this path. It will never be forgotten or overlooked.

Special thanks to Lou Aronica for believing in this story after only one page was written. I can't fully express my gratitude for your faith in my ability to tell a story and for your guidance in drawing the most of this book and out of Mark's pain. Thank you, and here's to many, many, more.

Jess, you may be new to my life, but you sure aren't new to my soul. I look forward to the discovery and adventure that awaits us, and for the countless hours I'll now be able to play like a kid with Sadie. All in. Let's do this.

To Jingle Jim and his uncanny brain of chess thinkings and mathings I'll never understand no matter how much he tries to "simplify" them: I thank you for most of a lifetime of friendship that is more brotherhood than friendship, and less frustrating by leaps and bounds than family. It takes a special bond to know you can trust that the other will never shout your name before they yell "Gardyloo!"

To Katie Moss of Katie Lynn Moss Photography, for a stellar eye, an artistic flair, and for the fabulous image used on this cover. Thank you so very much for everything.

And finally, a belated thanks to Gordon. You were a troubled kid who needed far more attention and guidance than you ever received. I know that now. I know you did the things you did because you never learned about boundaries or consequence. I know that no matter how your life ended, or how you got to that moment, that your heart and your friendship were never in question. I hope the Gordon of this tale—the Gordons of the world for that matter—can find the peace and redemption you never did.

ABOUT THE AUTHOR

Broadleaf Writers Association Founder and Executive Director Zachary Steele is the author of *Anointed: The Passion of Timmy Christ, CEO* and *Flutter: An Epic of Mass Distraction*. He has been featured by NPR, *The Atlanta Journal-Constitution*, *Publishers Weekly*, *Baby Got Books*, and *Shelf Awareness*, and was nominated for the Sidewise Award for Alternate Fiction. You can follow his ramblings on writing and life at http://zacharysteele.com/.